MW01534418

PRAISE FOR LAURENCE SHAMES' NOVELS

"Characters flashier than a Key West sunset and dialogue tastier than a conch stew."

— New York Times Book Review

"As enjoyable as a day at the beach."

—USA Today

"Funny, suspenseful, romantic, and wise."

—Detroit Free Press

"Smart and consistently entertaining."

—Chicago Tribune Book Review

"Delicious dark humor and healthy cynicism."

—San Francisco Chronicle

"Hilarious and always on the mark."

—Washington Times

SUNSET BLUFF

LAURENCE SHAMES

Copyright © 2024 Laurence Shames

All rights reserved.

ISBN: 9798873975594

DEDICATION

To Marilyn

She almost makes the day begin...

Oh, what a tangled web we weave, when first we

practice to deceive...

Sir Walter Scott

This above all: To thine own self be true...

William Shakespeare

PROLOGUE

S o these two ghostwriters walk into a bar...

I know, I know. It sounds like the start of a joke, and you're probably wondering if it's one you haven't heard before, and guessing that the punchline will be delivered in fifteen seconds or so, and hoping it'll be worth a laugh and that'll be the end of it.

Well, sorry, that isn't how it's going to go, because what happened from there was way more than a joke. A comedy, let's hope—a comedy of errors, some innocent, some not so much; a comedy about the things that inevitably go wrong when people try too hard to be other than who they are—but a mere joke it is not. A joke just tickles. A comedy also aches.

So this is a comedy about faking it, a farce whose details I'm only too familiar with, because one of the ghostwriters who walked into that bar on what I guess could be called that fateful afternoon was me. It's embarrassing to admit, but I was the instigator of the knuckleheaded scheme that seemed so awfully clever at the time. In all the convoluted bluffing and faking that followed, I was one of the bluffers. This sketchy behavior landed me in plenty of trouble, believe me. Damn near cost me my career. Could easily have cost me my kneecaps or my testicles. On the other hand, the escapade gave a thrilling spark to my love life, if only briefly, and not without leaving a hole in my heart. But at least I made it through with my sanity more or less intact. As for the other ghostwriter, my colleague if not quite my friend...well, let's not get ahead of ourselves.

So—how do I begin?

I guess I should start with the town where all this happened, namely Key West, Florida. Frankly, I doubt this particular story could have happened anywhere else. Not that there aren't other towns that have bars and writers and people who drink rather heavily in the afternoon. But I don't know of anyplace else that has so many bars and writers squeezed together on a rocky little outcrop maybe two miles by four. To shrink it down still further, there's only a certain part of town where writers are likely to live, probably about a mile on a side. Fully one-fourth of that square mile is taken up by Key West's famous above-ground cemetery which, by the way, also houses many writers. Within the close-packed neighborhoods reserved for the living, there are roughly eighty bars, and roughly seventy of them are frequented mainly by tourists. Which leaves around ten places where the locals go, and where the people without real jobs, such as writers, lay claim to the most desirable barstools and get a head start on the day's first round of cocktails. So, given the extreme concentration of writers and bars in that little corner of Key West, it was really sort of inevitable that, eventually, my colleague and I would walk into the same place at the same time.

It happened on a Thursday, maybe three-thirty or four in the afternoon. Whatever the exact time was, it was time for a gimlet. Not just any gimlet, but the way they make them at a dim little dive called the Eclipse Saloon, with muddled Key limes and smuggled Cuban sugarcane. Just in case you have an image of what a Key West bar is like—open-air, with a guitar player doing Jimmy Buffett covers, kids firing down jello shooters, women carousing in wet t-shirts—here's your opportunity to let that image go. The Eclipse is the opposite. No sunlight. No music. No slushies. The place offers a padded U-shaped bar, very generous pours, conversation if you want it, peace and quiet if you don't.

Anyway, I said before that my colleague and I walked in at the same moment. That was a slight exaggeration for effect. Sorry, occupational hazard. Actually, he came in thirty seconds or so after I did, just as I was ordering my drink, and we saw each other out of the corners of our eyes. This led to an awkward and, in retrospect, pivotal moment. Should I invite him to join me, or should I not? To be clear, we were not friends, not even close acquaintances at that point. We'd just happened to end up at a few of the same cocktail parties given way too often by the publishing crowd. We'd been introduced and I'm sure our professional creds had been mentioned in passing, but I don't think we'd ever exchanged more than a few scraps of conversation. My first impression, if I'd even had one, was that he was a clever guy but maybe a bit too literary for my taste. Then again, almost everyone at those parties was a bit too literary for my taste, so maybe that's just my problem.

In any case, I had a lot on my mind and I wasn't sure I felt like making chit-chat. Especially with a colleague who, by the nature of the business, was also a competitor. Or what if I felt like talking but he didn't feel like listening? Or what if he was meeting other people? Would he then feel obligated to include me? Generally, I'd rather be included out. What if I thought his friends were schmucks? What if they thought I was a loser who couldn't even find a friend of his own to have a drink with? What if the conversation got too bookish or was just plain boring and then I couldn't break away?

All these things went through my mind in a heartbeat. I mention them only as evidence of the many tiny and fleeting dilemmas we all face just getting through the day. Eggs sunny-side or over easy? The green shirt or the blue? Usually the choices we make turn out to matter so little that we don't even notice we've made a decision. But now and then...well, let's just say that life could have been so much simpler and safer if I'd just smiled and waved rather than smiling and flicking a wrist toward a barstool next to me, and by that wordless and badly thought-out gesture got the train wreck rolling.

Anyway, he stepped over, said hello, we shook hands, and he sat down. His name was Evan Briggs and it totally suited his looks. He was tall, lean, with neatly parted sandy hair phasing into a becoming touch of gray at the temples. He was wearing a dark blue polo shirt that worked well with his light blue eyes and he somehow got the collar to stand up straight so it cradled his neck. He was wearing pleated khaki shorts with a crisp but not too crisp crease. He ordered a martini and asked me how I was.

I said, "So-so," and asked the question back to him.

"About the same," he said.

We made some small talk until his drink arrived. Then we clinked glasses. "Cheers," he said, with a small sigh that verged on the theatrical. "I suppose I should be in much better spirits than I really am. I signed a new contract today. They want three more books from me. With an option for three more."

"Wow," I said. "Six-book deal. That never happens anymore. Congratulations."

I tried my damnedest to make this sound sincere and hearty, but come on, let's be real. *Congratulations* can often be an incredibly difficult thing to say, right up there with *I love you* and *I'm sorry*, and I don't think the tendency to choke on the word or to have your face cramp up from trying so hard to smile is unique to writers. It's human nature, right? Unless you're a total dick, you want at least some of your colleagues to do well. Just not too well in a way that reflects badly on you.

Be that as it may, at that moment it wasn't too much of a struggle to offer good wishes because it so happened I had some news of my own. Good news, even though it didn't seem to be making me any happier than his news was making him.

"That's an amazing coincidence," I went on. "I also picked up a gig today."

"Really?" he said. Did I detect just the slightest hint of deflation or annoyance in his tone, as if my announcement somehow took the gloss off his, as if he was the only writer allowed to get new work that day? Was there a whisper of a sneer in what came next. "Another Mafia bio?"

I guess I should mention that ghostwriting for the Mob has been my livelihood for quite a few years now. Back when I was based in New York, I sort of stumbled into doing books for wiseguys who wanted to tell their side of the story. The books were sold as autobiographies, and my name, which happens to be Richie Delinco, was never on them. Outside the publishing business, the Key West writers' clique, and a handful of social clubs in Brooklyn and Queens, no one's ever heard of me. I'm mostly okay with that. Mostly. But the problem is that I've been pigeon-holed with this Mob stuff. Editors don't seem to think I'd be capable of writing any other kind of book. Who knows, they might be right. But how can I ever prove them wrong if they keep me jammed up working as a ventriloquist for Godfather wannabes?

So I guess I sounded a little grumpy when I said, "Yup, another Mafia bio." I looked down at my drink and drank some. Probably more than I really meant to.

"Sounds great," he said.

Call me touchy. My first thought was that the comment was sarcastic and that the sarcasm was about as veiled as a bra from Victoria's Secret. I guess my hurt feelings showed, because Evan quickly went on.

"No, really, I mean it. I've always thought your projects must be a lot of fun."

"Fun? Okay, the first few maybe."

"But, I mean, they must be satisfying. You get to deal with real people. Colorful people. You give them voices. You're part of real events. There's so much life—"

"Death too," I put in.

"Of course. It's reality. That's the appeal. The meat. Frankly, I'm envious sometimes."

This took me totally by surprise, and it was at that very moment that I started liking Evan at least a little bit. Nothing like knowing a person envies you to make you feel more kindly disposed toward him. So I was determined to be gracious in return.

"Hell," I said, "I'm the one who should be envious. I'm grinding away trying to get these goombahs to express themselves in something resembling English, and you get paid to write bestselling fiction."

He came out with a refined little snort and took a deep pull of his martini. "Garbage," he said. "I get paid to write garbage. Tired plots. Wooden dialogue. Sex scenes where you don't know whether to laugh, cringe, jerk off, or just go wash your hands. All for the greater glory of a mediocre writer who's been dead for most of a decade."

I guess I should explain here that Evan is a slightly different subspecies of ghostwriter. He writes books for dead

6

people. At that time he was writing for a dead person named Harry Forest who, before he was killed in a heli-skiing accident somewhere at the top of Finland, had been cranking out a wildly successful detective series. The publisher, on hearing of Forest's untimely demise, sent out a reverent and touching press release but saw no reason to shut down the franchise just because its creator had been buried under twenty-six feet of snow. The company was in business to make money, after all. Did Mickey Mouse get canceled just because Walt Disney kicked the bucket? So they hired Evan to mimic the style and keep his mouth shut, and HARRY FOREST books kept making the bestseller list. The reading public either didn't know or didn't care that they'd been written by an impostor. Evan's name was nowhere on the cover. He remained as anonymous as I was. Both invisible. I guess that was a sort of bond between us.

In any case, I still thought it was pretty cool that he was getting paid to write fiction, and I told him so. The compliment backfired. It only made him gloomier. "I suppose," he said. "But is there anything of my own in these books? Zero. Anything I'm proud of? Almost nothing. Christ, I'm just so fucking bored with them. Have another drink?"

I hadn't been aware that I was ready for a second drink, but when I glanced down at my gimlet I saw that somehow it had disappeared. This has been known to happen with a first cocktail. I doubt I'm the only person who's ever had the experience. In any case, we asked for another round. It proved to be a bad idea.

We had just clinked glasses for the second time when the fateful words fell from my lips. That's a pretty hoity-toity figure of speech and I wouldn't ordinarily use it, but in this case it seems strangely accurate. The words just sort of softly bubbled out. I hadn't planned to say them. I certainly hadn't thought them through. I just heard myself say, "Well, maybe I should do yours and you should do mine."

7

Evan said, "Hm?"

"You know, I'll write your book and you write my book."

He sipped his drink and said nothing.

Recklessly, I blundered on. "Why the hell not? I feel trapped with my stuff. You're bored stiff with yours. Why not just switch?"

For the first time since he'd sat down, Evan smiled. It was a tight smile and not especially pleasant. It made his lips get flat as anchovies. "Amusing notion." He paused. "Impossible, of course."

I thought about it for a second or two. "Yeah, of course it is. Guess I was only kidding."

Truly, though, I didn't know if I was kidding or not. That happens sometimes, right? You say something really out there, something that probably should be disallowed, you see if it flies, then you sort of backpedal and say you were just kidding.

We drank in silence for a while after that. A few more people straggled into the Eclipse. A puff of salty, thick Keys air mixed with the A/C each time the door was opened. Behind the bar, ice was being shaken. A guy with a booming voice was complaining about how the fishing wasn't like it used to be and the seaweed stink got funkier every year.

Then, barely above a whisper, Evan said, "I wonder if it really *is* impossible. Really, why *would* it be impossible?"

I guess that was the first instance of us switching roles. I mean, I was the one who'd broached the preposterous idea, but suddenly he was the one leaning into it while I started seeing all the obstacles.

"Well, for one thing," I said, "I've never done detective fiction. You've never done a tough-guy memoir."

"So what? We've read some, right? We're professionals, aren't we? Ghostwriters, for Christ's sake. Not sounding like ourselves is what we do. This should be a breeze."

"But—" I began and got no farther. My misgivings couldn't quite keep pace with Evan's burgeoning enthusiasm.

"Your guy. Your subject. You met him yet?"

"No," I admitted. "Never. We were hooked up by an editor in New York."

"So he doesn't know you from Adam."

"Not by sight, no. All he knows is my name. He's coming down here in a couple days to start the interviews. No need for us to meet till then."

"And what about the editor. How often do you meet with her?"

"Meet?" The idea seemed quaint. "Evan, I haven't met with her since Covid. We don't even Zoom anymore. We send emails now and then."

"Same with mine," he said. "She works from home. Or Canyon Ranch. Or Paris. Who the hell knows where she works from? Months go by with zero contact. And you know what that means, my friend? It means we're free."

My scalp was feeling a little snug from the second gimlet and things suddenly seemed to be moving awfully fast. Just a few ounces of gin ago, Evan and I were cautiously sniffing each other out for signs of professional jealousy or bitchiness. Now he was calling me his friend and we were wobbling together on the brink of a very dubious conspiracy. Groping for some solid ground, hoping to slow things down a bit, I said, "I think maybe there's something you're forgetting."

"Namely?"

"We're under contract."

"So?"

"So, I signed on to write a certain book. You signed on to write a different book. If we don't write the books we said we'd write, but claim we did, well, not to be too harsh about it, it's kind of fraud."

This was intended to be cautionary but for some reason it had the opposite effect on Evan. It galvanized him. He swiveled on his stool and ran a hand through his sandy hair. After the brief mussing, every strand fell perfectly back into place. "Exactly," he said.

"Exactly what?"

"Look, don't you see?" He was leaning way forward on his elbows by now, almost like a cricket. "Fraud. The books are frauds to begin with. I'm writing as a dead man. That's a fraud. You're making it seem that some guy who can barely read or write suddenly bangs out a polished memoir. Due respect, that's fraud, too. So what's the big deal about adding one more layer of pretending?"

I wiggled my hands and got my lips ready to talk but I really couldn't find an answer.

Evan steamrolled on. "Or look at it this way. Everyone has a ghostwriter these days, right? Presidents. Princes. Prostitutes. Why should we be left out? Why shouldn't ghostwriters have ghostwriters? Actually, that's a nice postmodern touch, now that I think of it. Besides, as long as the books get written, you think the publisher gives a rat's ass who writes them?"

Well, I must admit he sort of had me there. So I settled for a stalling tactic. "Look, why don't we sleep on it—"

"And see if it still seems like a good idea tomorrow?" he interrupted. "But it won't. Of course it won't. Great ideas never seem like good ideas tomorrow. *Sicklied o'er with the pale cast of thought* and all that Hamlet stuff. That's why we should agree to it now. While it's fresh. While it's exciting. While it's making us happy. Come on, let's shake on it."

He drained his martini and held out his hand. I watched it dangle for a second or two. It was another of those awkward moments. Could I decently refuse a friendly handshake? Could I wimp out on something that had started as my own idea? Then again, it wasn't like I'd be signing anything in blood. I could back out in the morning. The whole conversation could easily be dismissed as tavern talk or maybe it would be forgotten altogether. So I shook his hand.

He smiled that thin-lipped smile again and I noticed something I hadn't focused on the first time. His light blue eyes had a disconcerting way of pulsing and flashing when he smiled, the pupils shrinking and expanding like the shutters on old cameras, and suddenly, too late, in the midst of the collegial handshake, it dawned on me to wonder if Evan Briggs might be a little crazy, a little too quick to skid from gloomy to glad, from reluctant to obsessed. Maybe not the best guy in the world to conspire with.

"Excellent," he said, and gestured to the bartender with the hand that wasn't hanging on to mine. "So it's agreed. Our deal. Let's have one more drink. A toast to our mutual success."

PART I

ONE

The following morning, much too early, Richie Delinco's cellphone rang. He was hungover and very groggy and it took some fumbling to free his hand from underneath the damp and tangled sheet to answer the call. "Yeah?"

"Yo, Richie, my man," said a gravelly voice with a heavy Brooklyn accent. "How the hell ya doin'? Everyt'ing okay wit' you?"

Richie rubbed his eyebrows and glanced at the dim louvered window at the foot of his bed. "Yeah. Fine. Sure. Who is this?"

"Come on. What're ya, kiddin' me? Like ya don't reconnize good people when ya hear 'em? Like ya don't know an ol' fren?"

"No, sorry, I don't."

"Ahh. Then I guess I mus' be doin' pretty good." There was a spasmodic laugh followed by a momentary pause. Then the New York accent was replaced by upmarket Connecticut. "It's me. Evan."

"Evan? For Chrissakes, man, you have any idea what time it is?"

"Not really. I mean, it's light out, right?" There was a faint rattling sound as of fiddling with a Venetian blind. "Sort of light, at least."

"It's ten after six. And what the hell's up with the Brooklynese?"

"Jus' gettin' inna character, *cugino*. Gotta know how to talk to these paisans, *capeesh*?"

"Yeah, but that isn't how you do it. Not like you have a hot mouthful of lasagna. You talk to them like human beings."

"I guess. But I'm just so revved up, Richie. I don't even think I've slept. Can't remember the last time I was this excited about a book."

Richie labored to prop himself on pillows and struggled through the fuzz of his hangover to recall the reckless words of the evening before. "The book. Right. Um, we're going to need to talk about that."

"Of course we are! A lot. There's so much I'll have to learn. So much background we'll both need to be filled in on. I'll speed-read a couple of your books, you can speed-read a couple of mine—"

"I don't speed-read, Evan. I don't speed-do anything. I like to go slow. I think things over."

"But there isn't time to think things over. Your subject—*my* subject—didn't you say he's coming down here in just a couple days?"

"Right. He is. But as for the rest, forget about it. It isn't happening. Go to sleep."

"What isn't happening?"

"The whole thing. The switch. Look, it was just a barroom fantasy. Letting off some steam. Good for a few laughs. But it can't happen."

"But you promised!" said Evan, with a suddenly boyish mix of indignation and hurt feelings in his voice.

"I didn't promise."

"You did."

"Look, Evan, we were bullshitting around in a bar."

"We weren't bullshitting. We were discussing. We were discussing and we made a plan. And we shook on it."

Richie said nothing, just rubbed a hand over his face and tugged at the edges of his eyes.

"Do you deny we shook on it?" Evan went on. "We shook on it, and a handshake is sacred. It's part of The Code, right? A man's word is his bond. A handshake is a contract. Come on, Richie, you've probably heard your goombah collaborators say that many times. I mean, Christ, you've probably put those exact words in their mouths."

"Okay, okay, I have," conceded Richie. "But look, these guys are mobsters. They're different. They live by all that Men of Honor stuff. Or at least they say they do. Makes 'em feel good about themselves. But it's their Code, not ours. It's not for regular people."

"Why the hell not? Why can't guys like us be Men of Honor in our own little way? Like by keeping our word, for instance?"

"Look, we were just chatting in a bar. Just trying to get through the day."

"Right. And what kind of day had it been? A day when we both felt crappy, when we both felt like drudges doing our same-old-same-old gigs. Then we had a glimpse of freedom, a whiff of change. And it felt great, didn't it?"

"Okay, yes. Briefly. But—"

"And, due credit, it was your idea to begin with," Evan said.

"Well, that's neither here nor there."

"You know what I think, Richie?"

Richie kept silent. He didn't want to hear any more of what Evan thought. All he wanted was a pee, a glass of water, a couple of aspirin, and a chance to go back to sleep.

Evan went on anyway. "I think you're afraid."

It was the most basic and ancient of taunts and it almost always worked. "Afraid? Afraid of what? Afraid we'll get caught and blacklisted and go broke and starve? Okay, I admit it. I'm a little bit afraid of that."

"Fine," said Evan, "but that's not all of it. The truth is you're scared of writing a different kind of book. Afraid you'll come up short. Afraid you'll fail."

"Evan, listen—"

"Hey, there's no shame in that. I'm scared too. Scared shitless, if you want the truth. But isn't that the whole idea? The fear. The stretch. Isn't that really what we shook hands about?"

Richie stared off at a corner of his bedroom, where the morning's first breeze had lifted an edge of the cotton curtain that hung in front of the louvered window. He watched it flutter for a moment. His eyeballs itched and he was very confused. Evan was manic, that much was clear, but that didn't mean he was wrong. Especially about the fear. That hit home. And even his pitch about the old-school sanctity of a handshake...Then again, it was widely agreed that only fools took dares and much of what his colleague had been throwing at him came down to a flat-out dare.

Finally, he said, "Evan, look, you're wide awake and I'm so not. It's an unfair advantage. So I'll make you a deal. You have any tranqs or sleeping pills around?"

"Sure, of course. Who doesn't?"

"How about you take a couple, maybe six or eight, sort of calm things down, and maybe we can have a chat this evening? Send me an address. I'll see ya later."

He clicked off without waiting for a reply, put a pillow on his head, and tried without success to get back to sleep.

TWO

It was already close to sunset when Bert the Shirt d'Ambrosia suddenly realized he hadn't spoken with anyone except the dog all day.

This was extremely unusual, as Bert was known all across Key West as the dapper old guy, a former New York *mafioso* as the open secret went, who would talk to anyone and everyone about any subject whatsoever. But now and then there was a day that lacked for opportunity. There'd been no one hanging around the pay box where, still in his burgundy satin bathrobe and scuffed-up slippers, he bought his morning paper. No gin rummy or shuffleboard games going on next to the pool at the Paradiso condo, the oceanfront complex where he'd lived for almost fifty years. No shopping that needed doing, not even a stroll to Fausto's for a head of lettuce. No incoming phone calls, not even one, and no good reasons or excuses to call somebody else. Just a very quiet, almost monkish, day.

Luckily he had the dog to talk to. The dog's name was Nacho, a chihuahua mutt and an excellent listener. Or at least he appeared to be because of the way his oversize ears would cock and swivel toward the sound of his master's voice, and the way his bulbous, glassy eyes would take on an alert and sympathetic gleam in response to whatever had been said. True, the conversations between man and dog were a bit one-sided; then again, so were many conversations between two people if you listened hard and thought about it.

In any case, it was late in the day and they were hanging out at Bert's favorite place in the whole wide world, a narrow slice of Smathers Beach known to locals as Sunset Bluff. The name itself was something of a bluff, as the spot was no grand promontory, just a slight rise in the rocky sand, barely high enough so that Bert, seated king-like in his aluminum folding chair with the criss-crossed yellow and white nylon straps, comfy in his forest green terry-cloth cabana set, could see over the heads of any tourists clueless enough to stand between him and the Atlantic Ocean.

Although the unobstructed vantage was a luxury, the place itself, by most measures, was really nothing special. There were many prettier beaches in the world, hideaways where the sand was finer and the water was clearer and took on more calendar-worthy arrays of color. But there was no place else that felt exactly like that modest little scalloped stretch of Smathers with its arc of coral boulders tip-toeing into the sea. Maybe it was just Bert's deep familiarity with the place that made it precious; maybe familiarity alone, with places as with people, bestowed a gloss that otherwise wouldn't shine as bright.

Though it's also true that there was no other place that smelled exactly like Sunset Bluff, with its mingled whiffs of salt and iodine and seaweed funk and coconut sunblock wafting from the water side, while from behind, where food trucks lined the promenade, came boardwalk smells of burgers on the grill and potatoes in the fryer and pizzas sprinkled with oregano browning in the oven; childhood smells that whisked together the present and the past and linked each fragrant sunset to the thousands of others that had gone before. Always the same and never the same. The bottomless toy box of jigsaw clouds, the tireless play of light on water, the sighing mix of relief and melancholy when the glare stopped challenging your eyes and dusk came creeping in.

Anyway, at that particular moment, Nacho was digging in the sand and Bert was looking down to watch him, wondering what the hell the dog was digging toward and how long it would take him to give up on ever finding it. So the old man didn't immediately notice the approach of his writer friend, Richie Delinco, who was only half a dozen steps away when he called out, "Hey Bert. I was hoping I'd find you here."

"Well, you weren't exactly playin' a longshot," the old man called back above the soft hiss of the wavelets percolating down through pebbles at the shoreline. "I mean, where the hell else am I gonna be?" He swiveled in his beach chair, his shrunken haunches squeaking slightly against the nylon straps, and held out his hand. "To what do I owe the honor of the visit?"

"Well, if you're not too busy—"

"Do I look too busy? I'm watchin' the stupid dog dig a hole. What's on your mind? Wanna sit?"

He gestured toward the sand. Richie eased down onto it. He was a wiry guy, no extra poundage. He had a nice head of curly brown hair that was just beginning to give up some real estate at the top of his tall forehead. He had hazel eyes with yellow flecks and a pliable mouth that smiled often though seldom as widely as a grin. He petted Nacho while the dog sniffed at his legs and licked the salt from his ankles. said, "Well, here it is. I'm suddenly in a kind of crazy situation with my work. And who else can I talk to? Hardly anyone but you even knows what I do."

"I get it," said Bert. "Not widely known on accounta you're anonymous. And what's the point a bein' anonymous if everybody knows? Hell, I wouldn't know either, 'cept that a few a your subjects, or authors a record I guess the lingo would be, happened to be guys I dealt wit' or in some cases former allies or even mortal enemies back inna day, but what the hell, forgive and forget if everyone's still breathin', so of course I took an interest. Now that I think of it, that's how you and me first met, right?"

"Yup," said Richie. "Seven years ago. I was doing *Bad Egg: The Benny 'Eggs' Falucci Story*. Remember, he came down here, took a suite at Harbor House. Asked you to sit in on a couple of interviews at first."

"Yeah, he was nervous," said Bert, bringing a red silk handkerchief up to his banana nose and giving it a good loud blow. "People are funny, right? I mean here's a guy that controlled the whole chicken business in the entire tri-state area. Wings, breasts, livers, eggs, the whole bird. He's got no compunction whatsoever about sendin' in a crew to make one big giant egg foo yong outta someone else's warehouse if he tries to muscle in, and yet this same guy is nervous about talkin' to a writer who goes maybe one-thirty-five, has no bodyguard, no crew, and goes around armed wit' nothin' but a pencil. 'Zat make any sense to you?"

Richie just shrugged and Bert continued giving vent to his pent-up love of talking.

"But I gotta say that you always did a fair and even touchin' job a bringin' out these knuckleheads' human sides, even Benny's, which can'ta been easy to do 'cause, let's face it, a coupla these clowns were real thugs and assholes, so I tip my cap that you broke through to find that little spark a decency that dwells in all of us, or at least we like to think it does, or at least it does inna movies, but then again, the question is, was it really worth diggin' through all the brutality and bullshit to find that little spark, dim and flickerin' though it may be, sometimes almost, whaddyacallit, extinguished altogether, like the way ya used to have to turn the old Zippo lighters upside-down to get a spark just before they were runnin' outta gas and sometimes it would burn your fingers...But wait, where were we goin' wit' this?"

"Um, I was trying to tell you about my work dilemma."

"Oh yeah, right. Continue."

Continue? Richie thought. Bert hadn't let him start yet. He fumbled a moment, then said, "Well, I have this colleague—"

"Male or female?" Bert immediately cut in.

"What's the difference? It's a colleague."

"Right, and last I looked, colleagues still came in different sexes, just like everybody else. These days I guess we're not supposed to notice that, or mention it at least, which, excuse me, happens to be unnatural bullshit. But you said you got a work dilemma, so I'm tryin' ta picture various scenarios. Male or female?"

"Male. Name's Evan. We had a few drinks last night. Hardly knew each other before that. Turns out he does a very different kind of ghosting. He writes novels for a dead guy."

"A dead guy needs novels written? I thought dead guys didn't need nothin' from nobody. I thought that was like the main advantage a bein' dead."

"What I mean is he writes books in the dead guy's name. For his publisher. Apparently the books still make a shitload of money."

"Even though the dead guy didn't write them?"

"Doesn't seem to matter."

Bert reached down, picked up his chihuahua, brushed the sand off its nose, and cradled it in his lap. After a moment's reflection, he said, "What a fuckin' world, huh?

25

The livin' can barely scratch out a livin' and the dead are rakin' in the cash. 'Zat make any sense to you?"

"Not really," Richie said. "But anyway, we had this conversation..."

The old man pursed his rather flubbery lips and listened intently to the retelling, rubbing Nacho's head like he was stroking his own chin. Then he said, "So lemme make sure I have this straight. You're both unner contract. You're both bored silly. And you're thinkin' maybe you wanna swap jobs but not tell no one."

"You got it."

"Innerestin'. Risky. Why not just tell people what you're doin'?"

"The publishers? They'd fire us in a New York second. They wouldn't believe we could pull it off."

"Doesn't say much for their faith in ya's."

"No, it doesn't."

"So, could you?" the old man asked. "Could you pull it off? I mean, ya got the chops to do it?"

Richie glanced off toward the horizon. The sun was taking on the illusory keyhole shape it seems to have for just a moment before it dips into the sea. He pulled in a deep breath and let it out slowly. "Well, that's the thing, Bert. I don't know if I do or if I don't."

"Guess ya wouldn't know unless ya try. Guess ya'd still be wonderin'.."

"Yeah. Maybe forever. So it's a tough one. This morning I thought the whole thing was way too crazy and I was totally ready to call it off. Then Evan sort of rubbed my face in it about being afraid to try something new. And I've been coming around more and more to admitting he's right. I'm scared. A novel? You know, nutty as it sounds, working with real live killers doesn't faze me. It's my comfort zone. I know where I am. But a blank page? Kind of terrifying. Then again, am I ready to lay down and admit I'm just a one-trick pony? Then again, what if I try a novel and I flat-out suck? So, do I go for it or not?"

Bert rubbed the dog between the ears and said, "Is that a whaddyacallit, rabbinical question?"

"Rabbinical?"

"No, wait, that ain't the word I mean. Rhetorical. Rhetorical is what I mean. So is it a rhetorical question or are you askin' my opinion?"

Richie pulled his legs in and squeezed his knees. "Well, I guess it's some of both. 'Cause the thing is, Bert, you're the only guy I know down here who has, let's say, some connection to the world I write about, so if I decide to go ahead with this, I might need a really big favor that probably isn't even fair to ask."

Bert stroked the dog and said, "Go ahead and ask it anyway. What's the worst that can happen?"

"Well, I might possibly need for you to sort of play along at some point."

"Play along?"

"Well, if I try to write the novel, that means Evan would be working with the Mob guy but pretending to be me, and if the Mob guy happened to be someone you knew—"

"Which it is," Bert casually put in.

"Excuse me?"

"Anthony Pisano, aka Tony Totes, the sports-bettin' king."

"How the hell you know that, Bert? It's supposed to be a secret."

"Well, it ain't. Not to me, at least. He called me a couple days ago. Said he's comin' down, we should get together for old times' sake. Said somethin' about a book. I thought he meant, ya know, like a bookie book. Now it all makes sense. Sorta."

"Jeez, Bert, you could've told me that before I went into my whole long story."

The old man smiled, mainly with his very black eyes that were settled very deep within their crinkly sockets. "Richie, there's a sayin'. *When you listen, you learn. When you talk, you teach.* I wanted to learn your situation."

Richie looked off to the west. Pink rays with yellow swaths between them were fanning out from where the sun had been. "Well, doesn't much matter now. My situation's over."

"Over?"

"Look, Bert, if Tony Totes is a friend of yours, I can't ask you to—"

"What? Play a little trick on 'im? Like no one's ever played a little trick on me? Lemme ask ya this. You write Tony's book or this guy Evan writes the book. Anybody get hurt?"

"Not as long as the book gets written."

"Awright then, what's the fuckin' problem?"

Richie gestured in the air but couldn't quite find words.

Bert said, "Ya want my opinion what the problem is?"

The younger man kept quiet.

"My opinion, even though ya didn't ask to hear it, is that you're lookin' to get off the hook for this terrifyin' novel that you don't know if you can write, and you're thinkin', *Here's my out. Bert's gummin' up the works. So I guess I'll just get back to doin' the stuff I been doin' all along that I'm sick and tired a doin' but at least it don't scare me.* But you know what, my friend? That line a reasonin' doesn't get it done, 'cause I'm not gummin' up the works and I'm not gonna be the excuse for you not takin' a shot at this. I'm in."

"But Bert, what if—"

"No buts, Richie, and no what ifs. You asked me to play along and I'm tellin' ya I'll do it. True, I sometimes get mixed up, and now and then you might have to remind me who's pretendin' to be who, and whose name is what, and that type a thing. Not sayin' I'll do perfect. But if you're lookin' for an out, ya better find a different one, 'cause I am totally on board wit' this."

And he held out his crinkly hand for another one of those Men of Honor handshakes—well-intentioned clasps that suddenly seemed to be stretching up toward Richie's throat and making it a little tough to breathe.

THREE

Evan was sipping gin on his narrow porch and gazing across his three-foot swath of front yard that gave on to a very narrow roadway and the cemetery just beyond it.

His house—a weatherbeaten two-story Victorian partly paid for by proceeds from his Harry Forest knockoffs but with years of mortgage payments still to go—was on Angela Street, which bordered Key West's graveyard on its northern edge. In a town of skinny pavements, Angela Street was one of the skinniest, less wide than some basketball players are tall. It was one-way, since it wasn't nearly wide enough for two cars. It was barely wide enough for one car and a bicycle, unless the car was one of the many in town that had already had its side-view mirrors scraped off in collisions.

The street was too skinny to accommodate a sidewalk, and the spiked black iron fence of the cemetery abruptly rose up on the far side of the ribbon of asphalt. Immediately beyond the fence loomed the blockish and ever-taller family crypts of people with names like Benavides and Cardenas and Acosta, Cuban clans that had first moved to Key West centuries ago to make cigars. Generations lived and died; as more descendants needed to be laid to rest, there was nowhere to go but up. So the vertical family plots grew high as houses and, in certain seasons and at certain times of day, threw jarringly distorted rectangles of shade across the street. At dusk, the west-facing sides of the mausolea glowed lavender.

When Evan first moved into the house on Angela, he'd had some misgivings about having all this death so close at hand—so close that at moments there was a faint tang of formaldehyde in the tropic air. But he soon came to see the advantages. Such considerate neighbors. No loud parties. No screaming bedsprings. A contemplative setting. A perfect place to write.

Or to sip gin on the porch, as he was doing when Richie came rattling down the street on his old blue clunker of a bike to keep their promised appointment. It was almost full dark by then. Streetlamps buzzed as they powered up. Swarms of gyrating moths instantly gathered around them. "So you found the place," Evan called down.

"No problem. Great street when you're not stuck behind a funeral," said Richie. He leaned his bike against a palm and stepped onto the porch. "How you doing? Got some rest, I hope?"

"Some."

"Calmed down a little, maybe?"

"A little. Have a drink?" He waggled his gin.

Richie said, "Think I'll go a little easier tonight. Glass of wine maybe?"

"We can do that."

He went into the house. Richie sat down in a wicker chair and looked across at the crypts. He estimated that, if he leaned forward, he might be able to touch a couple of the nearest ones with the tip of a good-sized fishing pole.

Evan came back in a moment with a big glass of cold white wine in one hand and a short stack of his ghosted books in the other. "Cheers," he said, passing the wine to his guest. Presenting the books, he perkily added, "Okay, let's get down to work. These should be enough to get you started."

Richie thanked him and put the novels on a small table between the porch chairs. Evan looked faintly miffed. "Aren't you even going to look at them?"

"Not this sec. I think there's a few things we need to clear up first."

"They're quick reads. You'll pick up on the formula in no time."

"I hope so. But before we jump into that—"

Evan jumped in anyway, talking very fast. "Look, here it is in a nutshell. The hero is this guy Rock Brittenham. Ass-kicker when he has to be, but mainly more of a charmer. Gets people to tell him things they shouldn't tell him. Sometimes he finds clues. Standard stuff, matchbooks and such, nothing too high-tech. Don't mess with politics or AI. It's an older audience. Sometimes the hero overhears things or just runs into lucky coincidences. You're allowed three of those per book. Settings? Always upscale. Manhattan. Bay Area. The Hamptons. On a yacht can work. Private jets are good. There's always a damsel in distress, of course, though occasionally she's evil. Usually rich, but for a nice twist, maybe only acting like she is. Rock and the damsel end up in the sack within six or seven chapters. Maybe on the first try they get interrupted on the brink. Gunshots from the garden, a scream from the jacuzzi, whatever. Builds tension. Sex scenes run two, three pages, maybe four if you're really having fun. Big tits are fine but don't get too anatomical. Now, as to the villains—"

Richie raised a hand and finally managed to break in. "Evan, whoa, whoa, take a breath. You told me you've calmed down."

"Well, I have, but just a little bit. Which is good. If I calm down too much I get into a funk, and that's no fun for anyone, believe me. Fine line sometimes. So anyway, about the villains—"

"Can we please save the villains for another time?" Richie pleaded. "There's something we need to talk about, or there aren't going to be any villains or any damsels or any clues or any books. It's a whole new wrinkle."

Evan ran a hand through his perfect hair and it fell back perfectly into place. For a moment he seemed to hang suspended between his own rambling momentum and his intrigue at what he'd just heard. He swirled his gin and smiled his thin-lipped smile. Finally he said, "Whole new wrinkle? Aha, the plot thickens. I love it when that happens. So talk to me."

Richie sipped some wine before easing in. "Ever met a guy named Bert the Shirt?"

Evan pulled his brows together. "Met him, no. Heard of him, sure. I think maybe he's been pointed out to me around town a couple times. Ancient guy with a jumpy little dog? Always wears these big-collar shirts that were the height of wiseguy fashion maybe sixty years ago?"

"Yup, that's him. Former Mob guy. Happens to be a friend of mine. And I told him just a little while ago what we were thinking about doing."

"You told him? What the fuck were you thinking? The whole idea is that nobody's supposed to know."

"Right. Except for him. Listen, I had to run it by him. He knows me. And he also happens to know the guy who's coming down here to tell me—or you—his life story. He might even sit in on some of the interviews. The ones with you, not me, as the interviewer. So he could blow our cover in a heartbeat."

"Shit," said Evan. His eyelashes drifted downward and instantly he seemed to swing from revved to crushed.

"Except he's promised me he won't. Not on purpose, at least."

"Excuse me?"

"Look, Bert's a player. A busybody, some might say. Loves to be in the thick of things. And he picked up right away that I'd be very disappointed in myself if I didn't try at least to write your stupid book for you. So he says he'll play along. He'll be our ally."

Evan perked up again at once. "An ally! Nice. Not anything I would've counted on. But nice."

"Unless he blows it," Richie cautioned. "Accidentally. I mean, the guy's intensely old. He gets mixed up sometimes. He admits it. There might be slip-ups here and there. Wrong names, whatever. Might be touch-and-go sometimes. Might call for some improvising. It's just an extra factor."

"Texture," Evan said. "Adds texture."

"Yeah, okay, fine, if you insist on getting all fancy and literary about it. I was thinking more it might get one or both of us beat up or killed if this Mafia guy figures out we've been jerking him around. What happens to your texture then?"

35

A gibbous moon had floated up above the graveyard. The looming crypts took on a chilly silver sheen. Flecks of granite sparkled on the headstones. Blithely, Evan said, "Well, I guess we'll find that out, won't we?" He drained his gin. "Now, let's move on to the delicate question of what sort of person can or cannot be used as an acceptable villain these days..."

FOUR

Over the next couple of days, Richie skimmed through Evan's books, and Evan skimmed through a few of Richie's, and a sort of unconscious mimicry began to settle in, shaping the rhythms of the phrases that ran through their respective heads. Each was drifting toward writing like the other before either had actually set down a word.

And in the meantime, Anthony "Tony Totes" Pisano had arrived in Key West with a very beautiful and much younger woman in tow.

Bert the Shirt picked them up at the airport. This was completely unnecessary, as Tony's hotel, the Flagler House, was barely a mile from the terminal and there was always a rank of Key West's bright pink taxis loitering at curbside and eager for a fare. But Bert had an unshakable if somewhat archaic sense of what was right and fitting, and he believed that when a colleague came to town, he should be picked up in person. Besides, the old man's vintage El Dorado, with its rusted-in-place convertible roof and porous fluid reservoirs that left sticky blue stains on the cement floor of the Paradiso's garage, hadn't been started in a couple of weeks, and Bert was happy to have an excuse to fire up the clattering V-8 and go somewhere, even if it was only two, three minutes up the beach and two, three minutes back again.

But even a short drive was a drive, and not to be approached without due ceremony. So Bert had to dress the dog and himself appropriately for the occasion, in matching snap-brim racing caps and vests with a pattern of checkered flags. He dug out his tattered driving mocs from the bottom of the closet and found his perforated calfskin gloves in the same drawer where, more out of sentiment than in expectation of near-future use, he kept his .38, which he fondled briefly before tucking it back behind some balled-up pairs of knee-length Ban-Lon socks. When all else was done, he made sure that Nacho's goggles were comfortably settled over his bulging eyes. Then they headed down to the garage, at which point Bert remembered that he'd left his car keys in the condo, so he had to go upstairs again, and when he got there he felt like he had to pee. So all in all, getting ready for the ride took six times longer than the ride itself.

But it was worth the trouble just to see that Tony Totes, an old-school guy himself, really did appreciate the gesture. "Bert, you old bastard!" he called out in a husky voice as the El D pulled up to the curb in front of baggage claim. "It's damn nice a ya to do this."

"What?" said Bert, as he slowly unfolded himself from the driver's seat and lifted himself to standing, the goggled dog held in the crook of his arm. "An old friend comes to town and I'm gonna stick 'im in a cab like a stranger?"

"Old friend" was an overstatement, a stylized formality. Still, the two men moved toward each other and embraced, the puzzled chihuahua lightly squeezed between their ribs. They stopped short of kissing on both cheeks, though there was a sort of vestigial move in that direction, evidence that traditions don't vanish all at once, just gradually lose their oomph.

Over Tony's shoulder, Bert caught a glimpse of his beautiful companion. She might have been twenty-six, twenty-eight. She had softly gleaming black hair that was parted in the middle and cut so that it followed the lovely descending arc of her jawline. Already dressed for the tropics, she wore silky pink shorts that didn't cover much of her thighs, which were lightly tanned but with a suspect tinge of salon magic from up north. She wore a sleeveless white top that caressed her collarbones before being cantilevered by her chest and then hanging straight down without encountering more torso. Her eyes could not be seen behind big sunglasses, but her full mouth held an expression that seemed to come so naturally to attractive younger women; not exactly sulky, but managing to convey a brooding mix of impatience, boredom, and a tireless wish to be someplace, anyplace else.

As for Tony Totes, who must've been into his early sixties by then, he was only average in height but gave a bigger impression because he was so thick. Not fat, but burly everywhere; meaty chin, thick neck, wide shoulders, heavy arms. In the midst of the old-school hug, Bert felt as if he was being swallowed up and he wondered if the dog could breathe. It was a relief to ease back into the bustle of the loading zone.

"Safe to put the bags inna trunk?" asked Tony, indicating one small and one very large suitcase near the curb.

"Safe?" said Bert.

"Ya know. No bodies or anything in there these days?" He gave his companion a wink, though he still didn't bother to introduce her. She looked more embarrassed than amused.

Bert felt himself briefly flushing but made a quick recovery. To the lovely young woman, he said, "Such a kidder, your boyfriend."

She said, "He's not my boyfriend."

Bert shifted the dog to his other hand. "Husband?"

"Please."

"'Scuse me, sorry. My mistake."

There was a moment of awkward silence as Tony Totes lifted the bags and put them in the trunk. Then he gave Bert a sideways look and said, "You really don't remember her?"

Bert pursed his lips and thought. He forgot a lot of things but he doubted he would have forgotten such a striking young woman. Besides, when might he have met her? "No," he said. "I'm sorry but I don't."

Tony broke into a wide proud smile. "My baby daughter, Darla. You were at her christening."

"Christ," said Bert, "has it really been that long?"

The only answer was the slamming of the trunk.

FIVE

Tony Totes had booked a penthouse suite. It had two big bedrooms with balconies that hung over the swimming pool and looked out to the ocean. The bathrooms were marble and full of fluffy towels and equipped with shower heads that could spray a person everywhere at once. The living room had white sofas and a wet bar and sliding glass doors that disappeared entirely so you could almost feel like you were on a ship. It was a swanky place but Darla had zero interest in being there while her father and his ancient buddy shot the breeze about the good old days, so she went out for a walk.

She passed under the Flagler House's *porte cochere* and followed her nose to the ocean, the matted seaweed being particularly thick and ripe with salty funk that season. She rounded the pickleball courts with their motley assortment of braced and bandaged players, then traced out the snaking walkway through Higgs Beach, where a couple of guys lay passed out in the gazebo next to the No Sleeping sign. She crossed the foot of White Street pier, heard *bocce* balls clicking across the way. Relieved to be on her own, savoring the breath of a hot breeze on her shoulders, she hugged the shoreline as the road curved toward Smathers Beach and the sidewalk broadened to a promenade that teemed with life. People were jogging, skating, cruising past on a dozen different kinds of locomotion gizmos. Bicycles slalomed by, dodging people toting paddleboards and cornhole goals and coolers. Tossed footballs arced over the crowd; veering frisbees found their targets.

Up ahead, at what seemed the vortex of the happy chaos, a convoy of assorted food trucks lined the curb and pumped an orgy of entangled smells into the humid atmosphere; their customers, with the urgency of salt-air appetites, weaved back and forth between the seawall and the jam-packed service windows.

Darla had almost made it past the vendors when she had a yen, as irresistible as it was sudden, for a Sno-Cone. Grape. Sweet. Like from childhood. Gooey with cold, thick syrup at the bottom of the cup. The most innocent of pleasures. So joyous and powerful was her craving at that moment that it blotted out all else and she made a beeline for the Sno-Cone truck without looking left or right...

...Just as an old blue clunker of a bike was rattling toward her at a pretty good clip. Its rider hit the brakes and swerved to avoid her but didn't quite manage it. The tip of his handlebars just barely caught the crook of her elbow. The momentum spun her rather gracefully around, almost as in a dance move, then she did a sort of slow-motion fall onto the concrete of the promenade. The bicyclist lost his balance from the glancing impact and wound up sprawled on his side with the bike resting mostly on top of him, its back wheel lazily turning. Their faces ended up very close together and eye to eye at sidewalk level.

"You okay?" he asked after a breath or two, his cheek comfortably nestled against the warm pavement.

"Pretty sure," she said. "Yeah, fine. You?"

"Yeah, no worries."

She eased up from the ground. The strap of her sleeveless top had come off one shoulder. She demurely put it back in place. Her left knee was slightly skinned, faint lines of red tracing out the scrape. The scrape was oddly fitting: Childhood pleasure, childhood hurt.

"I'm really sorry," she said. "It was all my fault."

He had lifted the old bike off his leg and was rubbing away some grit from his scratched-up elbow. "No, it was my fault," he countered. "I shouldn't go that fast through here. "

"But I never even looked," she said.

"No big deal. Bike's been through worse." He straightened out its bent metal basket.

"Well, I'm still sorry. I just suddenly had this crazy craving for a Sno-Cone. Like out of nowhere."

She shrugged. He shrugged back and looked at her. Then he tried to stop looking at her but couldn't. The black hair. The pretty jawline. Her inadvertently fetching gesture as she'd straightened out her blouse. That innocent scraped knee. He'd never been much of a pick-up artist. Generally too shy or doltish to seize the moment. Had gone home many nights thinking about what he might have said but didn't. So he was quite surprised when he heard himself say, "Still want one?"

"Hm?"

"A Sno-Cone. I kind of feel like one myself. Can I get you one?"

She hesitated. She'd often been offered drinks in bars, of course. Accepting them had led to mixed results at best and she'd more or less sworn off that way of meeting men. But a Sno-Cone? In broad daylight? With a guy who'd been so nice about their mishap? She felt her guarded expression unlocking toward a smile and said, "Sure, why not? Thanks. Grape if they have it."

He leaned his bike against the seawall. She sat down, swung her legs over, and looked out at the twinkling ocean. In a moment he was back with two cones, a grape and a lemon-lime. He handed one to her and they did a silent clink with their paper cups. "Cheers," he said, "I'm Richie."

"Darla," she said as she lowered her face toward the first raspy lick of ice.

"Nice name. Don't hear it often. What brings you to Key West?"

"What makes you think I'm not a local?" she fired back.

He took the opportunity to glance at her silky pink shorts. "Dressed too nice. Haircut's too good. Skin's not leathery enough."

"I guess I should take that as a compliment."

"Yeah, you should, though I'm sure you've had nicer ones."

She let that pass. "Actually," she said, "I'm here with my father."

"Ah. Nice. Family vacation."

"Family's a stretch. It's just the two of us. My Mom took off when I was little. Anyway, I didn't want to come."

"Why not?"

"Just didn't."

"So why did you?"

She nibbled some ice, lifted her cone a few degrees to get the syrup flowing. "Pop sort of bullied me into it. No doubt with good intentions. I think he's trying to keep me away from a guy up north I've sort of been dating."

"Sort of?"

"Well, yeah, sort of. It's been sort of casual, and this guy wants to make it much more serious, and I'm not sure I want that but then again I'm not totally sure I don't."

"How come?"

"How come?" she echoed, and took a contemplative lick of her Sno-Cone. "Well, okay, you asked, sorry if it's TMI. But this guy, Ralphie his name is, okay, maybe he's not the brightest guy in the world, but he's very cute and in his own way he's very sweet and caring, and he works for my father, which is both the good news and the bad news all rolled into one."

"Could get complicated," Richie said.

"Very. Ralphie handles a lot of let's say sensitive jobs. Things most people couldn't do. My father trusts him enough for that but at the same time doesn't seem to think he's good enough to date me. Do you find that weird at all? Who knows, maybe fathers always think that way about their daughters. This guy's not good enough, that guy's not good enough. But let's be real. I work at a sunglass kiosk in a shopping mall on Staten Island. Who'm I going to meet, Mark Zuckerberg? So, anyway, I think my old man's keeping me away from Ralphie, or keeping Ralphie away from me is I guess more like it. So now I finally make it to sunny Key West, which I guess could be a lot of fun except I'm with dear old Dad and what I'm supposed to do is sit around this big hotel being bored to death while he tells his life story to some writer."

Richie snapped his head up from his Sno-Cone. *Tells his life story to some writer?* Unthinkingly, he said, "Oh, so your father is..." Then he caught himself. Under the cockamamie deal with Evan, he himself should know nothing about a man named Tony Totes. A slip like that could scotch the whole ruse. Covering his hesitation with a quick cough, he finished the sentence. "...a celebrity?"

"Not hardly. Just a guy with an interesting life. Interesting to him, at least." She picked off a little patch of ice that didn't have syrup on it and swirled it around and around the scrape on her knee. "Boy, does that feel good," she said. "Takes the sting right out. Anyway, yeah, he's doing some kind of book. With a ghostwriter. Funny, I think that guy's name is Richie, too. Richie Defiore? Dipinto? Something like that."

"Delinco," Richie said, and instantly wished he hadn't.

"Oh, you know him?"

"Um, no. Sort of. I mean, all the writers who live down here sort of hear about each other."

"Oh, so you're a writer, too?"

He sucked some ice as a stalling mechanism and tried to shake off the feeling that he'd already started digging a hole that had no bottom and from which he would never emerge. "Well, yeah, I am."

"This town has a lot of 'em, I've heard."

"Can't swing a cat, as the saying goes."

"What kind of stuff you write?"

Another perilous moment. He couldn't very well say *Mafia memoirs.* "Oh, this and that. Right now I'm doing fiction. I don't like to talk about it much."

"Understood. Sorry. I guess you creative types tend to be mysterious."

Suddenly realizing that mysteriousness might be a point in his favor, Richie just gazed soulfully past the matted seaweed and out toward the horizon.

After a moment's musing, Darla went on. "Actually, I've sort of been wondering if maybe my father has in mind to try and line me up with this writer guy. It's the kind of thing he'd do. Like he knows better than I do what's good for me. He keeps telling me he's heard good things about this guy. That he's smart, trustworthy, that kind of thing. Guess that's the other half of why he leaned on me to come along. Keep me away from Ralphie, fix me up with someone he thinks would be classier."

Meaning Evan? thought Richie. *Evan pretending to be me? And therefore becoming Dad's top candidate?* It seemed totally unfair. Looking to level the playing field, he said, "Sounds so retro. I mean, practically medieval. You really want your father picking boyfriends for you?"

"Well, no, I don't. Course I don't. But it's not like I've made such great picks on my own. Made some lousy ones, in fact."

"Who hasn't?" said Richie. "But hey, I might like to point out that if you think a writer might possibly appeal to you and maybe even meet your father's standards, whatever they happen to be, you've already met one, namely me, and with zero help from Dad."

She gave him a sideways glance and smiled. Her teeth were faintly purple from the syrup. He knew that, if they kissed, her lips would be cool and grapey and a little bit sticky. But it didn't happen. Not then at least. She just said, "True, I have met one, and all on my own, and he seems pretty nice."

He said, "Well maybe, if it gets too boring listening to Pops talk on and on to this ghostwriter, maybe you and I could spend some time together."

"Maybe. I just don't know. I'll have to see how it goes."

"And I guess you'll have to wait and see how much you like the other guy. The one who's come highly recommended."

"Look, I'm not trying to be a tease, I promise. It's just that, well, you know, it's complicated."

"Oh, believe me, I know it is. But can I call you, text you sometime?"

She thought it over for a moment. "Better if I get in touch with you." She drained the last of her Sno-Cone, flattened the empty cup and put it on the seawall next to her, and took out her phone. Fingers poised on the keyboard, she said, "Number?"

He gave it to her.

"And what's your last name, Richie?"

"De...um, Briggs."

"DeBriggs?" she said. "Dutch? Belgian?"

"Sorry, just Briggs. I had a little syrup in my throat."

"Okay. Richie Briggs. Got it."

She put the phone away and swiveled around on the seawall. "Guess I should be getting back."

He fumbled for something, anything, to say to have a few more moments with her. He looked down at her knee. "Bleeding's stopped. That's good."

"Just itches a little," she said. "Something to remember you by."

"You'll get in touch?"

"I'd like to. We'll see. Thanks for the Sno-Cone."

She stood, and as she was rising she gave him a sort of fly-by kiss on the cheek. The kiss was so light and cool and happened so quickly that he almost wasn't sure it had happened at all. Without looking back, she headed down the promenade toward the Flagler House hotel. Richie watched her until she vanished in the swirl of joggers and skaters and swimmers still glistening with ocean water.

SIX

Evan's house on Angela Street was flanked by a narrow plunge pool that he had dubbed the Dip of Death because of its slightly macabre position in relation to the cemetery.

The pool wasn't quite grave-deep, but it was close. When Evan stood in it his eyes were at the paw level of the dogs that sauntered down the pavement barely arm's length away, beyond a battered and porous privacy fence that afforded almost zero privacy. Above the low fence loomed the blockish mausolea whose diagonal shadows carved the pool into triangles of sun and shade. So a living person with his feet very nearly six feet under would have to crane his neck steeply upward to gaze upon the unburied dead in their ghostly condominiums. There was just something cockeyed, vertiginous, upside-down about it. Something that appealed to Evan's darker side. He spent a lot of time in the pool.

He happened to be standing in it, elbows splayed across the apron tiles, studying up on one of Richie's books, when Richie himself pulled up on his dented bike, clambered up the porch steps, and hammered on the front door.

"It's open," Evan called out. "Come on in."

Richie stepped through the small living room and out to the pool by a side entrance. He saw the book that Evan was holding and it very fleetingly dawned on him that he'd never before actually seen a fellow human reading anything he'd written. Not on a plane. Not on a beach. Never. Seeing it now gave him an odd tingle and an instant's dizziness. It would be a stretch to call it an out-of-body experience, but he felt as if he was confronting some former part of himself, both alien and familiar, a sort of mini-me, not an offspring exactly, more like a thought-bubble that had swelled and burgeoned and finally floated off to claim its own existence in the world. Gesturing toward the volume, he said to Evan, "Enjoying it?"

"You know, it's really not bad."

"I'll take that as a rave review."

"I mean, it rings true. You can pretty much believe it was written by a semi-literate thug."

"Very kind, thanks."

"No, really, it's a compliment. The voice, the authenticity. It can't be easy to do that."

"Well, it isn't. And I'm glad you've noticed, because you're going to get your own shot at trying it starting at 9 am tomorrow."

"Tomorrow?!" said Evan, his body suddenly twitching so that water sloshed over the pool apron and dampened the cover of Richie's book. "I thought I had another day or so to prep."

"Well, you don't. Tony Totes arrived today. Bert picked him up a couple of hours ago. He's at the Flagler House and he's expecting me—meaning you—tomorrow morning."

"Shit," said Evan, getting jumpier by the moment. "I wanted to study more, get the accent down. Besides, what should I wear?"

"Wear?"

"I was thinking of picking up a shiny shirt, maybe sharkskin pants, some pointy shoes."

"Evan, you're not auditioning to be an extra in a movie. You're a professional writer doing a job. Just wear what you wear. Just be yourself."

The man in the pool pressed his thin lips together and frowned down at the shadowed water. "Richie, has it ever dawned on you that maybe I don't exactly know how to be myself? That maybe the whole concept is wasted on me? That maybe that's why I'm a ghostwriter? I need a role. I need a model."

"So all right, all right, get a shiny shirt if it makes you feel more comfortable. But skip the shoes. They'll look ridiculous. And let go of this whole Central Casting thing about who these Mafia guys are. They're people. Not exactly like you and me but not that different either. They have emotions. They have reasons for what they do. Their feelings can get hurt just like yours or mine. Keep that in mind and you'll do okay."

Evan looked only slightly reassured. He lifted himself out of the pool and started toweling off.

After a pause, Richie went on. "Now, there's one slight complication I need to fill you in on."

"I know, I know. The thousand-year-old friend you blabbed to. With the neurotic little poodle."

"He's not a poodle. He's a chihuahua. Name's Nacho.

You're supposed to know him. Remember that. But, actually, this is a different complication."

Evan rubbed the towel over his scalp and hid his face in it for a couple of seconds. "Another one already? Jesus Christ, Richie, what now? What the hell am I letting myself in for?"

"Look, you were the one who was so gung-ho."

"And I still am. I am. I'm just panicking a little bit right now. Part of the process. Happens every time. I'll get through it. Deep breaths, deep breaths...Okay, what's the other complication?"

"Tony Totes has a daughter traveling with him. She happens to be drop-dead gorgeous. I met her this afternoon."

"You met her? But—"

"But I'm supposed to stay out of the way. I realize that. Look, this was an accident. I ran her over."

"You—?"

"With the bike. On the promenade. Nothing major. Anyway, we got up from the ground and had a chitchat. This was before I realized she was Tony Totes' daughter, you understand. I mean, how could I know? I thought she was just one more pretty tourist. So it came out that my name is Richie, and then it just sort of came out I'm a writer."

"Oh, you had to mention that, didn't you? *I'm a writer. Ergo, I'm cool.*"

"Look, it's not like I just blurted it out—"

"No, no, I'm sure it just happened to come up. But why do we even bother to tell people we're writers? I mean, we all do it, right? And it always backfires. *Writer? Really? How interesting!* Then people ask your name. Then they ask humiliating questions about what have you written that they might have read. Then everyone's embarrassed and starts looking for an exit. Why don't we just say we make dry cleaning bags or coffin linings or something? Or why don't we just keep our mouths shut?"

Richie gazed off at the dusk while waiting out the rant, then said, "Well anyway, we were chatting and she happened to mention that her father was here to do a book with a guy whose name by coincidence is also Richie, Richie Delinco. Then later on she asked me *my* last name, so, since mine was already taken, I had to think of something fast, so the first thing I thought of was borrowing yours. So she thinks my name is Richie Briggs."

"But that's absurd," said Evan. "There is no Richie Briggs."

"Well, now there is. And if Darla—that's her name— ever finds out who I really am, I'll look like a total schmuck. Not to mention that our little book swap will be finished, maybe ditto our careers. Just thought you should know."

Evan took that in while shaking water from his ears. His body was bisected by the shadow of a crypt. It gave a sort of Harlequin effect.

After a pause, Richie said, "Oh, and there's one other part of it."

Evan sighed. "Why am I not surprised?"

"Her father, who seems to be the controlling type, apparently has it in mind to fix her up with this writer, this

Richie Delinco, who he's heard lots of good things about from friends. So she might be inclined to fall for this guy, who by rights is me, but she's going to think it's you. You follow?"

Evan wrapped the towel around his shoulders and sat down in a slatted chair. "I think so. It's twisted, almost operatic, but I follow."

"Well, just remember that I'm the one who came recommended, not you, so if she cozies up you to please her Dad, it would be bullshit."

Evan said nothing to that, but seemed to brighten a bit and started blithely humming as he continued drying off. The humming annoyed Richie and he said, "Evan, look, I don't even know if women are your thing—"

Casually, with his head cocked at a coy angle, the other man said, "I sort of take it on a case by case basis."

"Ah. Okay. Good for you. Very modern. But in the current case, I saw her first and I happen to be pretty smitten by her looks and attitude and the scrape on her knee, so I'm asking you to keep your distance."

"Scrape on her knee?

"From our collision. She got one on her knee. I have one on my elbow. They pretty much match. It's sweet."

Evan shrugged and flashed one of his anchovy smiles. "Very touching. But how and why the hell should I keep my distance? If I'm working with her father and she happens to like me—"

"I saw her first, Evan. And I'm asking you nicely. And we've done the Men of Honor handshake and all that other bullshit."

"I believe that Men of Honor would accept that all is fair in love and war."

"She and her father are here because of me, Evan."

"Are they? They don't really know you. A little bit by reputation, maybe. Basically they're here to meet someone named Richie Delinco. That's all they really have to go on, right? The name."

"Right. But it's my name, not yours."

"Not at the moment it isn't. We're switching, remember? At your instigation. So maybe it'll come down to the importance of being Richie." He swept the towel off his shoulders and turned his attention to drying his feet, one toe at a time. "Meanwhile, I very much look forward to meeting this goddess with the scrape on her knee. Sounds quite sexy."

SEVEN

Unlike Evan, Richie had never quite got around to buying a house. Never quite got far enough ahead with his savings. Never quite trusted that the next gig would come in soon enough to cover payments. So year after year he kept on renting a small yellow bungalow in a compound on Watson Street, one of those dusty and unglamorous byways off of Truman Avenue that hid its slow but steady gentrification behind rickety grape-stake fences and the occasional rank of rusted appliances stacked at curbside.

The compound itself consisted of half a dozen mismatched cottages arrayed around a palm-shaded courtyard with a shared hot tub and pool. Clothing was optional. Over time, Richie had noticed that it was almost always the people you really didn't want to look at who just couldn't wait to strip in public. Men or women, it really didn't seem to matter. The less photogenic the body, the more of it was bared to the sunshine, the salt-and-chlorine breezes, the neighbors' captive eyeballs. Why? Was it purely about freedom and courage and lack of inhibition? Was it a passive sort of in-your-face aggression, a demand to be accepted hairy warts and wattled chins and all? Or was it just a way of saving on laundry detergent? Who could say with human beings? And, in Key West at least, who cared?

In any case, the compound suited Richie pretty well. Tourists and transients came and went, providing a sort of bite-size sample of what was already a miniature town at the dangling tail-end of a continent. There were young and old, black and white and brown and yellow, straight and queer and indeterminate, people on the lam and people on the make; people looking for a second chance, or a third, or fourth; people seeking ecstasy or oblivion; people who had no idea what they were seeking, determined only that it be as different as possible from what they were used to...

Which, now that he thought of it, was the exact same blinding impulse that had pushed Richie into this loony arrangement with Evan. Just wanting something different. What he'd failed to consider at the start was that different didn't necessarily mean better, or even necessarily just as good. It just meant something else, a change for good or ill; and that vague notion, change, was very seductive in a whorish kind of way. It wasn't a promise; it was just a come-on, a tease. Why had Richie been seduced by it? The realization was gradually dawning on him that the culprit was ingratitude. Losing sight of how good he had it; that was his mistake and his transgression. He got paid to do stuff he mostly enjoyed and believed he was good at. Yet he'd allowed himself to grow bored with his work, even though he knew that getting bored was basically a failure of imagination. That self-indulgent boredom, in turn, made him at least temporarily ungrateful for what he had. So he'd glommed onto a shot at novelty and was kicking himself about it now.

As he strolled through the compound courtyard, trying not to look at a hirsute fat man who was floating balls-up in the pool, he was nursing his regrets and thinking about how simple things might have been. He could have kept his commitment to write a book with Tony Totes. There would have been no fakery required, other than the inherent fakery of writing other people's memoirs. And he would have been hanging out with Darla every day. Of course, he hadn't yet known Darla existed. Then again, no one ever said that human regrets were limited to the rational.

He let out a silent sigh as he opened the door of the yellow cottage. He put up coffee, cleared his wobbly desk, and prepared to take a crack at writing Evan's Harry Forest book, a twice-removed made-up tale with an improbably unflawed ass-kicker of a hero who always solved the case while having sex on yachts and in penthouses with fit yet buxom women who never failed to be aroused and also carried designer handbags. Richie tried to persuade himself that the project might be fun. Any kind of writing *could* be fun, after all. But this one sure as hell didn't feel congenial.

Then again, maybe he was just plain scared.

EIGHT

At nine the next morning, Evan, equipped with a notebook, pen, and digital recorder, rang the doorbell of the fancy suite at Flagler House. He was wearing black pants, an acceptably shiny long-sleeve shirt from the '90s that he'd rummaged from the back of his closet, black loafers that weren't quite as pointy as he'd hoped but still buffed up to a pretty good sheen, and Ray-Bans.

His collaborator opened the door wearing rumpled shorts, a faded polo shirt that clearly hadn't been folded when it went into the suitcase, and those shapeless terry-cloth slippers provided by decent hotels. Extending a hand, he said, "Hi. You must be Richie. Thanks for coming."

They shook, and Evan said, "Yup. Richie. That's me. Nice to meet you, Mr. Totes."

The other man looked slightly puzzled. "My last name isn't Totes. It's Pisano. Generally I just go by Tony. Tony's good enough."

"Sorry. Guess I'm just a little nervous. Always happens at the start of a job."

"Ah, don't worry about it," Tony said. "Come in, come in. We got a friend over, I think you know him. And you can meet my daughter. We're just finishin' up breakfast. Want some coffee?"

"Sure," said Evan, as the host led the way through the foyer and into the living room, where a room-service table had been set up in front of the disappearing sliding doors. Empty bread baskets and used plates with smears of egg yolk or edges of waffle on them stood before an unblemished background of flat green ocean. In one chair sat a very old man, resplendent in a burgundy silk shirt, feeding croissant crumbs to a chihuahua nestled in his lap.

Summoning his nerve, Evan launched into his bluff. "Hello, Bert," he said. "Good to see you again."

Right on cue, the old man replied, "Always a pleasure, Richie."

Emboldened, Evan pushed his luck. He bent down close to the level of Bert's lap and said in a baby-talk singsong, "And how is little Macho today?"

"His name's Nacho," Bert corrected.

Trying to cover up, Evan sing-songed to the dog, "And you're a macho little Nacho, aren't you?"

The dog seemed bored by the wordplay. It ate a few more crumbs then turned its face toward its master's crotch.

Evan lifted his gaze from the unamused chihuahua just in time to see a pretty young woman who might have been rolling her eyes. He couldn't be sure if she was really rolling her eyes or if it was just his unease that made him think so. But there was no doubt that her eyes were a deep violet and a very striking complement to the jet-black hair that followed the sweep of her jawline. She was wearing a hotel bathrobe, sashed at the waist, open at the throat, the lapels discreetly but not prudishly converging as they descended toward her breasts. Her legs were primly crossed and she had a Band-aid on her knee. Evan had to agree with the real Richie that there was something oddly enticing about the little scrape.

"This is my daughter, Darla," Tony Totes was saying. "I hope you won't mind havin' her sit in with us sometimes."

Evan flashed what he hoped was an ingratiating smile. "Not at all."

"And I hope she won't find it total torture listenin' to me talk so much."

She snugged up her robe and said, "Oh, no, I'm sure it'll be fascinating."

Bert slurped some coffee and said, "Nice, the way you did that, Darla."

"Did what?" she purred.

"Put in just that little hint a sarcasm. Not too heavy. Just a little whaddyacallit, facetiousness. Spices up a conversation. Keeps a little edge on. Nice."

Tony let that pass, poured Evan a cup of lukewarm coffee, and motioned him to sit on one of the plump white sofas. On an end table next to him was a copy of *Bad Egg: The Benny "Eggs" Falucci Story*. Evan's eyes flicked over at it, as writers' eyes are always drawn to books.

"The editor gave me a copy," Tony said. "Told me it was pretty good. Sorry, but I haven't got around to reading it yet."

"Me neither," Evan blundered.

Tony didn't know if he was joking. "But you wrote it, right?"

Recovering, Evan said, "Oh, yes, sure. What I meant is that I haven't read it again since publication. Busy with other projects, you know."

"Sure," said his host. "Understandable." He eased himself down into an armchair opposite and rubbed his hands together. "S'okay. Let's go. Let's light this candle. How the hell we start?"

Evan fussed a moment with his gear, then said, "Do you mind if I record us?"

Tony looked at Bert.

Bert pursed his rather flubbery lips. "Well, I'll say this much—it's nice that he asked. Feds never useta ask. They'd just bug a guy's house, sneaky like, and all hell'd break loose. Remember Paulie Castellano? They bugged his house, caught 'im sayin' incriminatin' things, not to mention screwin' the maid which, excuse me, was between the maid and him, but he shoulda gone somewhere else to do it, not right there where his wife lived, which was just flat-out wrong behavior, so he hadda get rubbed out for the greater good, which perhaps would not a been necessary wit'out the whole world could hear the bedsprings creakin' while he's boppin' the maid courtesy of the bug the Feds put in. Which is a long waya sayin' that maybe ya should nix this recordin' stuff, as it ain't exactly risk-free."

Tony nodded and told Evan, "Sorry. Ixnay onna recording."

Somewhat shamefacedly, as if it were a rejected sex toy, the ghostwriter stashed the recording device and took out pen and notebook. "Well, okay, we'll muddle through the old-school way. So, for starters, maybe you could tell me why you want to write this book."

"Why? Why the hell would anybody wanna write a book? Because I'm broke."

Darla said, "Oh, come on, Dad, you're not broke." She gestured around the lavish suite. The motion of her arms gave a sway and a surge to the lapels of her robe. "I mean, look at this place we're in."

"Okay, okay, not broke broke. But a helluva lot closer than I used to be. And this fancy place, don't jump to rash conclusions. I'm keepin' up appearances heah. Maintainin' a level of dignity and comfort that I and my family have become accustomed to—"

"Airbnb would've worked for me," Darla put in.

"—and that burns through a helluva lotta cash, of which I have a lot less than I useta have."

There was a slightly awkward pause, then delicately, cautiously, Evan said, "And is that something you'd like to talk about today?"

Darla said, "Of course he wants to talk about it. He talks about it all the time. No need to pussyfoot around like a TV shrink. Just ask him a question."

Evan steeled himself and said, "Okay, Tony, why do you have a lot less money than you used to have?"

"Now we're gettin' somewhere," Tony said. He leaned forward in his chair, rearranged his rumpled shorts between his thighs, put his elbows on his knees, and raised an index finger. "There's a few different reasons. But the biggest one, I can give it to ya in two words. Legalized bettin'."

Bert snorted. "Taxable bettin' is what ya mean."

"Fuckin' A," said Tony Totes. "Exactly. Taxable bettin' put in place by a buncha greedy hypocrites is drivin' my business straight into the ground. Throwin' good people outa work. Costin' them their livelihoods. And why? 'Cause a handful of corporate types greased the palms of a buncha politicians and spent a lotta money on publicity and started yammerin' about how we needed to 'clean up' sports bettin'. Clean it up, my ass! It wasn't dirty to begin with. It was a straightforward business operation. People laid bets with us. If they won, we paid 'em. If they lost, we didn't. What's the fuckin' problem?"

Bert said, "People bitched about the vig."

Evan said, "Vig?"

Bert said, "Sorry, um, Richie. I thought you mighta been familiar with the term from your previous endeavors. The vig is the extra ya gotta pay back when ya borrow to lay bets. Some people found the rates, let's say, excessive."

"Sometimes yes, sometimes no," Tony admitted. "But ya know what the real problem is with the vig? Just the sound of the word. It don't sound legit. We shoulda just called it interest. Like the banks do. Like with credit cards. Ya looked at your Visa statement lately? What're those late charges up to? Twenty-nine percent or somethin'? Tell me how this is different from the vig?"

Darla said, "Well, for one thing, Dad, Visa doesn't send a guy to your house to break your knees with a baseball bat if you miss a payment."

"Honey," said her father, "you've seen too many movies. Has something like that ever happened in the history of the world? Look, I'm not gonna sit here and say it hasn't. But it's very rare. It almost never comes to that. Why?

Because there's been a lotta talk along the way. A lotta tryin' to work things out. Face to face. Man to man."

"Yeah," said Bert, "the human element. The personal touch. Ya have a longtime bookie, he kinda gets to be a friend. Ya have some drinks, ya shoot the shit, ya swap advice. I mean, look, it's mainly a business arrangement, and business arrangements have been known to go sour, but inna meantime—"

"Inna meantime," Tony Totes picked up, "ya got someone ya can talk to. That's what's so fuckin' wrong about this so-called legal gambling. The company gets their cut. The government gets its cut. But the people part is shot to hell. A computer tells you if you won or lost. A computer tells you when your credit's all used up. But the problem is that the computer has no heart, gives no slack. Is the computer gonna give a rat's ass that maybe you got a car payment due this week but if the bettin' thing can wait till the following payday, then maybe it'll all come right? Is the computer gonna put a friendly hand on your shoulder and tell ya like a pal that there's no end in sight for your losin' streak and maybe y'oughta chill for a while?"

"Jeez," said Darla, "I never realized bookies and bag men were such white knights."

"Okay," said her father, "make fun of what I been doin' to put bread onna table for us all these many years. But look, I ain't sayin' we're saints and I ain't denyin' that there's some pricks and sadists inna business. But the truth happens to be that we worked out a pretty good system that gave jobs to a lotta guys and that allowed a lotta people to have a lotta fun and plenty of thrills from something they really enjoyed, namely bettin' on sports, and that the government said was evil and they shouldn't do. So what happens? We build this industry—which has its flaws, I admit it—but we build it up to where it's hummin' right along, and then these suits and politicians change their tune and say bettin's fine an' dandy as long as they control it and skim a nice percentage, so they do an end-run around us and muscle us out. That sound fair to you?"

The question hung a moment as Evan tried to catch up on his note-taking. He'd been scribbling furiously the whole time but still felt he was falling hopelessly behind. Feeling like he needed to contribute something, anything, to the conversation, he said, "So, on balance, would you say, with Lear, that you are a man more sinned against than sinning?"

Tony pulled his eyebrows close together. Then he swiveled around to look at Bert. "Who the fuck is Lear?"

Bert rubbed Nacho between the ears but could only shrug.

Evan said, "Doesn't matter. He's a foolish king in Shakespeare."

Tony said, "You callin' me a fool?"

"No. No. Not at all. That isn't what I meant. It's just—"

Tony waved away the fumbling explanation. "Don't worry about it, Richie. I ain't touchy. Besides, it happens to be true that I am a fool sometimes. Like I said before, the legalized bettin' bullshit ain't the only reason I'm goin' downa tubes. A big part of it is my own mistakes."

Evan flipped to a fresh page of his notebook and said quite softly, "Can we talk a little bit about that now?"

Darla said, "There he goes again, sounding like a TV shrink."

Her father said, "Darla, you really aren't helping."

She said, "Sorry," then got up from her chair, tightened the sash of her robe, and padded off barefoot to her room. The band-aid on her knee crinkled and uncrinkled as she walked.

Evan fought the urge to turn his head to watch her go. He said to Tony, "So you were saying..."

"Right, about my dumb mistakes. Mainly, they had to do with gettin' too chummy with my high rollers, trustin' guys too much, lettin' things get too personal."

"But they *were* personal," Bert put in. "That was the whole idea back inna day. Ya didn't deal wit' robots. Ya didn't deal wit' strangers."

"True. And the thing is, I really liked and respected mosta the high-end guys I dealt with. I'll be honest—a lot of 'em I looked up to. I'm a guy from the streets, let's face it. These were doctors, lawyers, Wall Street guys, guys with connections, fancy educations. Hangin' with 'em made me feel pretty damn good about myself. Maybe I'm a putz for admittin' it, but so be it. Eatin' steaks with these guys, havin' their private phone numbers, gettin' through onna first ring when most people couldn't reach 'em at all. Kinda puffed me up. Reminded me I was a player."

"Which is a helluva lotta fun," said Bert, "'cept that sometimes players get played."

Tony Totes nodded in sad agreement. "That pretty much nails it. I got played. Not often. Most guys paid up and everything was peachy. But a coupla guys, one guy in particular, really screwed me. Took advantage of my easygoin' nature. Took advantage of what I thought was a friendship. That's what hurts. I really useta like this guy. Charming. Real sport. Always picked up tabs. Witty. Kept everybody laughin'. I was laughin' too, till he stiffed me for three million bucks."

"Three million bucks!" Evan said.

"Biggest line a credit I ever gave anyone. That's how much I trusted this guy. And why wouldn't I? He made plenty of dough. Even if the bets went bad, he could cover it. At least I thought he could. I mean, the guy was very successful, famous even. So he strung me along and he strung me along, and the debt went from a million bucks to two, then to three, and I finally started gettin' nervous. I'd mention repayment and get nothin' but smiles and excuses. So gradually I get to realize that I've been a total sucker, which is a feelin' no one likes 'cause it makes ya feel like a real schmuck, so then I got pissed off, and especially pissed off because of how much I useta admire this guy. So at some point, even though it kinda tore me up, I decided it was way past time to take some action."

"Action?" said Evan. Caught up in the story, he'd forgotten about taking notes and just sat there with the pen dangling in the air. "What kind of action?"

Tony leaned farther forward in his chair and dropped his voice a notch. "Whatever needed doin'. Unnerstand, once a debt goes that far bad, ya can't do things half-ass."

"Ya'd lose your whaddyacallit, credibility," Bert put in. "Lose your credibility, you're toast."

"So ya do what needs doin' to collect the money," Tony said. "And if it turns out that the money isn't there to be collected, ya make an example of the guy as a reminder to others what the rules are."

Evan squirmed on the sofa and said, "So, um, did you get the money back?"

"Not a penny."

"So...so...if you don't mind...if it's okay to ask..."

"Come on, man, spit it out. Did I have the guy roughed up? Did I have him killed? No to either. Was I was ticked off enough that I coulda done both? Yeah. Woulda been sad for old times' sake but also necessary business-wise, not to mention satisfyin' after all the takin' advantage and treatin' me like an idiot. But anyway, I didn't get the chance. He died too soon. And with no help from me."

Bert said, "Talk about a lose-lose situation. The guy dies wit'out you get either your satisfaction or your money."

Tony shrugged. "Shit happens. Weird shit. Really weird sometimes. Guy goes on vacation. Goes skiing, gets buried in an avalanche. What're the fuckin' odds?"

The pen slipped out of Evan's hand. "Avalanche?"

"Yeah. Seven years ago, somethin' like that. Made the paper one day. Up in Norway, Sweden, some freezin' place like that. Buried alive. Whole mountain on top of 'im. And there went my three mil. My bankroll still ain't recovered."

There was a brief silence, though whether it was in honor of the dead man or in mourning for Tony's shrunken bank account was impossible to judge. The moment passed, then, delicately and cautiously, Evan said, "I think maybe I remember that story. Ran in the *Times*. The guy who stiffed you. Was he by any chance a writer?"

Tony gave Evan a sideways glance, his mouth curled in distaste but with just a hint of sorrow at the outside of his eyes. "Yeah, as a matter of fact, he was. Writer. Charmer. Liar. Deadbeat. Name of Harry Forest. Lookin' back, I shoulda been less nice and offed him when I had the chance. Sometimes I still wonder why I didn't."

PART II

NINE

Under the grimy low ceiling and hideous fluorescent lights of the Customs and Immigration hall at JFK, a seemingly endless snaking line of inbound air passengers was being herded through a maze of stanchions by a small army of sleepy-eyed guards with walkie-talkies. It was mid-afternoon, the time when the European flights swooped in all at once like a flock of giant geese. Visitors from France got jumbled in with Croats, Italians chatted amiably with Scots, Spaniards kicked along their carry-ons side-by-side with disapproving Swiss.

Among that day's gaggle of invading flights was Finnair 1313, non-stop from Helsinki. And among the first-class passengers who seized a mini-headstart in joining the immigration queue was a man whose passport identified him as a Finnish national named Henryk Faarsti. He was traveling alone, a robust though not young-looking man with a leonine head of silver hair just long enough to gather into a small knot at the nape of his neck. His face was bigger than most faces and commanded attention by its very scale. The forehead was tall and broad; the straight, thick nose descended from it with only a hint of a bridge. The eyes were so wide-set that they almost seemed to wrap around his temples. The cheeks were not jowly, but weathered and folded so that they gave an impression of great volume.

Like most of the people waiting in line, he held his passport in his hand. It had a dark red cover that said Suomi, which is what the Finns call Finland. It didn't look too new and it didn't look too old. It had a few visa stamps but not too many. It was an excellent forgery and had cost ten thousand dollars.

Many people on the crawling immigration line seemed frustrated and impatient. Henryk Faarsti felt otherwise. Seven years gone, what did a few more minutes matter? Besides, the more pressing the crowds, the less scrutiny per customer. When his turn finally came, he wordlessly handed the fake passport to an agent. He held his expression neutral and looked straight at the camera lens. He was asked a question he pretended not to understand. He gave an answer in what might have passed for Finnish, a language no one speaks. He was waved into the country, ready to reclaim his life as Harry Forest.

He took a taxi into Manhattan and headed for the Carlyle, his favorite haunt from the days when he'd breeze in triumphantly from his Sag Harbor home for meetings and assignations in the City, fully confident that his visit would be the top item on the agendas of his publisher and editor, that A-list lunches and dinners would have been booked for his enjoyment, and that no one would mind, or admit minding, the disruption to their schedules.

He had no idea how much the world had changed.

At the hotel, the service was adequate, professional, neither more nor less. There were no familiar faces among the bellhops or the front desk clerks. Time and a pandemic had changed the guard; his own supposed demise, though fraudulent, had erased him from many people's memories. So he should not have been surprised that it occasioned no fuss when he signed the register. Still, he was secretly abashed. He tried to persuade himself that this newfound anonymity was a great relief. He didn't believe it for a second.

He went up to his room, took his shoes off, and poured himself a Scotch. Then he plumped his pillows and lay down on the bed to make a phone call he'd been looking forward to for months, to his former editor and sometime lover, Emma Newton.

She did not pick up, of course. She was a busy woman and not the type who answered calls from unfamiliar numbers, still less from a phone with a country code she'd never heard of. He left a message. "Emma? It's Harry. I'm at the Carlyle. Let's have a drink."

If the message was simple, it was also utterly outrageous. When Emma called back moments later, her voice was shaky, mostly with anger. "Who the hell is this?" she demanded.

"It's Harry."

"Harry who?"

"Come on, Emma, how many authors and lovers named Harry you got by now?"

"Is this some kind of sick joke? I'm not finding it funny at all."

"Emma, calm down. It's Harry. Harry Forest."

"Harry Forest is dead."

He sipped some Scotch and allowed himself a brief laugh. "So the story goes. But I assure you he isn't."

"I don't believe you. Who are you and why the hell are you doing this?"

"Emma, Emma, how can I convince you I'm really me? Shall I remind you what you were wearing the first time we went to bed?"

"Stop this. Just stop, whoever you are."

"Dark green skirt just above the knee. Celery-colored ribbed turtleneck. Big earrings that matched the sweater. Underneath the skirt—"

"Enough! Stop! So it's really you, Harry, you rotten son of a bitch? You miserable, lying—"

"I knew you'd be glad to hear from me."

"Not exactly. But how the hell—?"

"I'll tell you all about it. When can you leave the office?"

"I'm not at the office, Harry. No one goes to the office anymore. I'm working at home in Brooklyn."

"Fine, fine, brave new world. When can you be here?"

"When can I be there? Just like that? Drop whatever I'm doing because you sashay into town after seven years of being dead?"

"Well, you have to admit it's kind of a special occasion."

"Listen, Harry, our little fling is very far in the past. We're clear on that, right? It was dead even before you were. Dumbest thing I've ever done."

"If it's any consolation, I've done dumber. But look, this is not a social call. It's business. There's a lot we need to talk about. Can you meet me? Please?"

"Please?" she said. "Not a word I've often heard from you. Maybe your manners are finally improving."

"Maybe, maybe not."

"And we agree it's only business?"

"Word of honor."

"Word of honor," she echoed. "Coming from Harry Forest? That's a good one. But okay, actually I've had the occasional daydream that someday, somehow I'd have the chance to talk business with you, Harry."

"Really? That's very reassuring."

"It shouldn't be. See you at Bemelman's in an hour."

TEN

In the little yellow cottage in the Key West compound, Richie Delinco was plugging away at the novel that Evan Briggs had contracted to write under the name of Harry Forest. So what did that make Richie? Pinch-hitter for a pinch-hitter? Third author twice removed? In any case, a bluffer.

But at least he'd made a start. He'd boldly typed the words Chapter One into a fresh computer file.

Then he got stuck. There were just too many decisions to be made. An unwritten novel was a tiny uncreated universe, an utter vacuum, an emptiness where not even time had started yet. There was no up or down, still less right and wrong. How the hell did you spark that nothing into being something? Daunted, he just sat there for awhile, looking out the old-fashioned louvered window, enjoying the way the angled panes of dusty glass cut the scenery into slices, and how you could make the slices seem to wiggle if you closed one eye and then the other and alternated very quickly.

After some minutes of studying this odd effect, he remembered he was supposedly working, and he tried again.

A few things, at least, he knew. There had to a beautiful woman with a tale of woe. She needed a defining detail or two. He could always fall back on the designer handbag shtick. Why not? But that already called for big decisions; would the handbag be the real thing or a knock-off? The genuine Chanel would take the story in a certain direction, the cheapo in another. The woman would appear to have been crying. But are the tears also a knockoff? Are they meant to fool the detective or the reader or nobody at all? If she's not the victim she claims to be, does that necessarily mean she's the villain? Is she a scheming manipulator or a selfless and long-suffering heroine who's protecting someone else? Is she looking for a savior or a fall-guy? What would Raymond Chandler do? For that matter, what would Harry Forest or even Evan Briggs do? Give these guys their props. At least they knew how to get beyond page one.

He pushed back from his desk and went to reheat his coffee.

That was when the text came in from Darla. She'd been cooped up all day long, the message said. She was dying to get out for a walk or maybe a swim. Any chance he'd like to join her? Maybe on the little beach right next to the Flagler House? The one with the gazebo?

He forgot about the coffee and texted back that he'd be there in ten minutes. He pulled on a very old bathing suit, turned off his computer, and watched with a mix of guilt and exultation as the screen went dark.

🌴 🌴 🌴

He found her sitting on a big striped towel laid out midway between the two sand volleyball courts, wearing a yellow sundress with thin straps that were tied in a bow at the nape of her neck. In front of her, the ocean was flat and milky green beyond its wreath of seaweed. Above, a scattering of small and fluffy clouds was providing momentary intermissions between brilliant episodes of sunshine. He looked at her a moment from a few steps away—the black hair shimmering, the bare shoulders taking on the first tender blush of sunburn—then walked his old blue bike across the lumpy sand and said hello.

Shading her eyes as she looked up, she said, "Thanks for showing up."

"Thanks for asking. I didn't know if you'd get in touch."

"I didn't know either," she admitted. "Sort of playing it minute by minute. Wanna sit?"

She patted the towel next to her. He lowered the bike onto the sand then eased himself down. It was a delicate operation. He didn't want his butt to land on the hot bare beach but he didn't want to seem too forward by squeezing in thigh to thigh. Carefully maneuvering, he came down so their hips were almost touching but not quite. A light breeze moved the fabric of her sundress. It tickled his leg. He caught the scent of her sunblock. Coconut and papaya.

"How's your knee?" he asked, gesturing toward the band-aid that had begun to curl at the edges.

"Oh fine, fine. How's your day going?"

"It sort of isn't," he said. "Just having a really tough time getting a book started. Mostly been staring out the window. Hibiscus flowers. Hummingbirds. Sometimes the birds almost disappear inside the flowers. Very pretty."

"Must be frustrating, though."

"Very."

She crossed her arms in front of her and sighed. "I kind of wish my father had a little more trouble getting his book started."

"Ah, so it's up and running?"

"And running and running and running. He just launched right in and talked for hours, with this old guy Bert sort of egging him on the whole time. He was still talking when I left. It's amazing how much people can talk about themselves. I listened for a while then got bored and went to take a shower. Came back, he's still talking. Went to change my clothes. Still talking."

Somewhat grudgingly, Richie said, "Well, give some credit to the writer. Takes a good interviewer to get someone to open up that much."

Darla curled her lips into a dubious expression. "You think so? I don't know. This guy mostly just sat there looking nervous with a notebook in his hand. Personally, I wasn't too impressed."

Best news I've had all day, thought Richie. But he graciously said, "Well, sometimes just keeping quiet is the best thing an interviewer can do."

"I guess. I mean, you seem to know a lot more about it. It's just that, well...I probably shouldn't say more. Small town and all. I mean, what if you and this guy end up being friends?"

"Friends?" said Richie. "Um, not too likely." The fibs were accumulating, and he tried to remember exactly what he'd previously said about his relationship with his co-conspirator. "I mean, I've heard his name. That's all."

"Okay, good," said Darla, "'cause if he was a friend of yours I wouldn't want to diss him."

Go ahead, thought Richie. *Diss him all you want! Diss him but good!* Instead, he said mildly, "Oh, don't worry about it. It's just between us."

"Well, okay then, just between us I didn't especially like the guy. I mean, there are some things that just don't quite add up for me. My father heard all this good stuff about him. Heard it from people he trusts. They told him he was very down-to-earth, a regular guy, easy to talk to, no bullshit."

Richie basked in the secondhand compliments and kept his mouth shut.

"Then it turns out," she went on, "that he doesn't come across as down-to-earth at all. He's too dressed up. He uses fancy words. Suddenly he's throwing in Shakespeare. I mean, what the hell does Shakespeare have to do with it? Honestly, he just kind of struck me as a phony."

"A phony?"

"A phony. A bluffer. I mean, he didn't really seem to know the turf. Dad and Bert started talking about the vig. He didn't know what it was. Shakespeare he knows but not the vig? He just seemed like an outsider. And a little bit of a snooty one."

"Doesn't sound like your father minded him."

"Who knows? Maybe he was too busy talking about himself to notice. Or maybe I'm just in a bad mood from being bored all day. The hell with it. Wanna go for a swim?"

The abrupt segue caught Richie a bit off guard. It took him half a beat to realize that going for a swim would also mean that Darla would remove her sundress. He said, "Yeah, sure. Sure." He clambered up from the towel and pulled his shirt off.

She stayed seated as she bent her head and untied the bow at the nape of her neck. He remembered reading somewhere that there are those who consider the nape the loveliest part of the female body—the graceful arc up from the shoulders, the secret skin usually curtained by the fall of hair. At that moment he was inclined to agree. Then she stood and gave one little shimmy so that the untied dress slipped down over her torso to her ankles. After that he couldn't pick a favorite part. She was wearing a turquoise bikini. By some standards—those of St. Tropez, say—it was actually quite modest. There was cleavage but no dollops of breast spilling from the outside edges of the top. The bottoms mostly covered the backside, except for those Cheshire-cat crescents where leg phases into buttock.

She caught him looking at her. If she minded, it didn't show. She smiled and stepped off the towel. "Christ, that sand is hot!" she said, and quickly yanked her foot back.

Then, to his surprise, she giggled and reached out, grabbed his hand, and tugged him along on herky-jerky tip-toe to the water's edge. With each step, the sulfury funk of the seaweed grew stronger, blotting out the fresher smells of salt and drying pebbles. At the shoreline, the wavelets didn't flow but viscously bulged beneath their cap of vegetation. Darla took a tentative step into the mix of water and weed. Her foot came back criss-crossed with red-brown ribbons; it looked like she was wearing some sort of biblical sandal. She said, "This is kind of yucky."

"Been pretty bad this year."

"Well, I don't want to sound like some princess from the City, but I don't think I can swim in that. How about we just go over to the pool?"

"Pool?"

"At the hotel. Our balcony looks right down at the deep end. You'll be my guest. Maybe you'll even meet my father."

"Um, I don't know if—"

"Chances are he'll still be up there yakking. Who knows, maybe you can meet the writer, too. Form your own impression. See if you find him as phony as I do. I'll be curious what you think."

ELEVEN

Bemelman's Bar, thank God, still looked the same, with its completely un-chic retro chic, its unapologetic whiff of *New Yorker* cartoon privilege. The gold-toned murals with their antic mix of city icons and fantasy animals still wrapped around the walls, the discreetly spaced banquettes with the creamy leather seats still lined the room, the immaculately polished Steinway still served as a totemic object, a shrine to sophisticated taste. True, the bartender was an unfamiliar face, but The Macallan 12-year tasted as it always had and the pours were nothing to complain about.

Harry was on his second drink, third if you counted the big one he'd had in his room, when Emma Newton was ushered in. She was wearing roomy black slacks and a rather baggy gray sweater. Her reddish-brown hair frizzed out just a bit at the sides. She wore owlish glasses on her bookish eyes that had been strained by years and years of reading and correcting. Her pale red lipstick was inexpertly applied. On the face of it, there was nothing remotely sexy about her, yet Harry had always found her improbably and mysteriously appealing. Maybe it was her wit, the sly and knowing look at the corner of her eye when she came out with a zinger. Or maybe it was a prurient curiosity about what this seeming goody-goody was thinking and feeling as she edited and improved upon other people's sex scenes. Then again, was it necessarily a powerful attraction that had led Harry to put the moves on Emma years ago, or only opportunity? With a man like Harry, it was tough to know, even for himself.

In any case, she was led to his table. He rose to hug her. She offered a handshake. His other arm fell limply to his side. They sat down. He told her she was looking wonderful.

"And you're looking...alive," she said.

"Surprising, isn't it?"

"That'd be an understatement, and understatement doesn't really suit you. Why the hell'd you do it, Harry?"

"Long story. Let's get you a cocktail. Still drinking Negronis?"

"Haven't had one in years. But maybe I will today."

He smiled. "Feeling a bit nostalgic, are we?"

"Not in the least."

A waiter came over and took her order. Harry signaled with rattled ice that he was ready for another.

"Well listen, I know it was very inconsiderate—"

"Oh, you think so?"

"—to leave you with a half-finished manuscript and all of that, but I had to disappear. Had to. I was in real trouble. Debt trouble."

"With all the freakin' money we were paying you?"

"It all went, Emma. I was paying serious alimony to four ex-wives."

"Would've been five if you did what you said you'd do and divorced the one you were married to when you sweet-talked me into the sack."

The waiter brought the drinks as these last few words were being said. He tried not to smile as he placed the glasses on the table.

"Cheers," said Harry.

"Up yours."

"Listen, I was going to divorce her. I would've been tickled to divorce her. I just ran out of time."

"Time for what?"

He leaned in closer. "Time to pay back my loan shark."

"Excuse me?"

"You see, you didn't know. No one knew. I hid it very well. I had a gambling problem. A big one."

At that moment she found empathy hard to come by. "Zipper problem. Drinking problem. I guess a gambling problem shouldn't come as a surprise."

"Come on, Emma, it's no joke. I got in way over my head. Got hooked up with a very major bookie. Cultivated him. Won his confidence. Used him, really, for the thrill of betting big. Got down three million dollars."

"Jesus Christ, Harry."

"I meant to pay it back. Of course I did. All I needed was one decent hot streak to turn it around. That's what they all say, right? But it wouldn't come. Lose, lose, lose. And I could feel my bookie losing patience with me. I could see it in his eyes. I could hear it in his voice. There started to be tough guys hanging around, sort of leaning in toward me—"

"So you did what any reasonable person would have done. You went to Finland and pretended to die in an avalanche."

At that, he couldn't quite suppress an almost boyish grin of satisfaction. "Emma, I make up crazy plots for a living. Why wouldn't I script one for myself?"

"Okay, okay," she said. "But it's one thing to do it in a novel, this was real life."

"You still think they're that different? Look, it wasn't as difficult as you probably imagine. I built up to it. For a few years I'd been siphoning off a little money into a Swiss account. Not much. Didn't have a plan in mind at the beginning. Just trying to stay a few shekels ahead of my ex-wives' lawyers. So I had some funds to work with. Then I just needed to find a few Finns who liked Swiss francs and had various abilities. Along the way, I made an interesting discovery: Finland is basically a one-price country. You need someone to seed an avalanche, it costs ten thousand francs. Someone to fly the chopper and confirm the tragedy? Ten thousand francs. Ditto for the guy who photoshops the death scene. Same payday for the coroner who stamps the death certificate without asking too many questions. Another ten thousand for the passport guy. So I was burning through a lot of cash. But you know what? All those bribes were roughly equal to what I was shelling out in alimony every month. Every freakin' month! With death it's one and done. Alimony canceled. Way better deal. Tough titty for the exes."

"Clever," Emma conceded, "if not very gallant. But what about the gambling debts? I don't imagine they got canceled quite so tidily."

He frowned down at his whiskey. "No, Mafia debts don't expire. That's a problem. It's the main reason I stayed away so long."

"So why'd you come back now? Why'd you come back at all, Harry?"

"Ever been to Helsinki, Emma?"

"When there's Paris? When there's Tuscany? Hell, no."

"It's dark four months a year. And do you know what they do for fun there? They roll around naked in the snow then whip themselves with birch leaves. I couldn't face another winter. Not holed up in some steam-heated apartment with one more Helga or Inge and a big stack of Aquavit bottles piling up in the recycling bin. Besides," he added rather sheepishly, "I finally ran out of money."

"Oh, poor you," said his onetime editor.

The bar had gradually been filling up. Men in business suits. Women dressed up for the theater. The piano player eased into the evening's first set. Gershwin, Porter, Kern. The glorious comfort of the standards.

Against the soft background of the music, Harry said, "And I actually got to miss writing."

"Ah," said Emma. "The lofty creative urge that often correlates with getting low on cash."

Ignoring the barbed tone, he said, "I started getting fresh ideas. Feeling excited to get back to work. And I came up with a plan. I'll live very modestly and use my advances to start paying down the gambling debts. I'm guessing my bookie will be reasonable after all this time."

"Sounds like a good plan, Harry. But what will you get back to work on?"

The question seemed to confuse him for a moment. "On Rock Brittenham, of course. I see the series still sells quite well."

"Nice that you've been keeping up with the bestseller lists."

"Of course I have. I've been in Finland, Emma, not on the moon."

"Well, even so, it seems that there's some industry news that hasn't made its way to you. And why would it have been of interest anyway, you being dead and all? But here's a little item I'm thrilled to be able to share with you, Harry. You don't own that series anymore."

"Excuse me?"

"You no longer own it. It isn't yours."

"What the hell do you mean, it isn't mine. I invented it. I created it. My name is on it!"

"True. And I'm glad you brought that up. You no longer own that either."

"Don't own what?"

"Your name. Harry Forest. It was part of the package."

He banged his glass down hard enough that the impact could be heard above the tinkling of the piano. "Package? Look, I don't quite get what it is you're telling me—"

"So I'll explain it as simply as I can," his former editor cut in. She took a small sip of her Negroni then moved it to the side. "You were still married when you supposedly died, so your fifth wife, Clarisse—"

"I remember her name, thank you."

"Well, she's doing everything she can to forget yours. She inherited the rights to all your books, of course. Could've been collecting royalties forever. But she wanted nothing to do with your work, your name, your so-called legacy. Nothing. So she just cashed out."

"Cashed out?"

"Took a lump-sum deal. Sold all rights back to the publisher in perpetuity."

"The bitch!"

"Now, don't be a sore loser, Harry. Besides, I don't think you realize just how much she hated you. I mean, figuring out about the little side-thing with me didn't help, though neither she nor I thought for a second that was your only slip-up."

Neither confirming nor denying, he said, "So how much did my little slip-ups cost me? Wha'd you pay her for my life's work?"

"Details are confidential."

"I don't give a rat's ass. Wha'd she sell me out for?"

"Ten million."

"Shit."

"Oh, and one more thing. As soon as the check cleared, she took off for Rio with her girlfriend. They sent me a picture from the wedding. Looked radiant. And now I think you're all caught up on industry news and gossip."

She fished the orange slice out of her cocktail and gave it a nibble.

For a moment he just sat there, stunned as if he'd been pummeled while tangled in the ropes. His right hand was cold and moist from clutching his glass. He rubbed his forehead with it. What had started as the soothing buzz of the bar had gradually mounted to an insufferable din. He felt a fleeting impulse to stand up and take a swing at the piano player. Finally he managed a rather twisted smile. "Another drink?"

She covered her glass with her hands. He ordered one for himself.

The first fresh sip more or less restored his calm and provided at least the illusion of clarity. "All right, Emma. So I've been outmaneuvered. I have no leverage. I get it. But the books still need to be written, right? How about I write them for you? Flat fee. I'll take half of what I used to get."

Slowly but inexorably, she shook her head. "Isn't happening, Harry. We have someone else. His prose isn't much worse than yours. He's less of a pain to work with. He meets his deadlines. And we're paying him about a tenth of what you used to squeeze out of us. It's just a good deal all around."

"Good deal except for me."

"Your own fault, Harry. Dead men make poor negotiators."

He tried to choke back an unseemly note of pleading. "Look, Emma, can't we work something out? I really need this job. I really need an advance. If I can't start paying down my debt—"

"Harry, I'm sorry for your problems. I don't quite know why I'm sorry, given what a shit you are, but I am. But I can't bail you out here. We have a long-term commitment to the other writer, and that's that."

"What's long-term mean these days?"

"Three books and an option for three more."

"Christ, that's like forever. What's his name?"

"Doesn't matter what his name is."

"Come on, what's his name?"

"Anonymous."

"Very funny. What's his goddamn name and where does he live? I need to talk with him."

"That would be completely inappropriate."

"Like I give a fuck what's appropriate or not? I'm trying to survive, Emma. If you can't understand that, maybe this guy will."

"So he'll give up his livelihood and the best gig he's ever likely to get just because you've made a mess of everything? He'll just step aside?"

"I have no idea what he'll do. Maybe he'll have the decency to be embarrassed that he's ripping off my series. Or maybe he could be...persuaded."

Emma finally swept off her owlish glasses and placed them carefully on the table. "Persuaded, Harry? Sounds a bit noir. Where you going with that?"

He fondled his glass. The truth was that, given his desperation and the alcoholic haze and the genteel chaos of the bar, he didn't quite know where he was going, but certain guilty thoughts linked by a certain brutal logic were starting to crawl and whisper in his brain. He owed his loanshark a lot of money. If he could somehow reclaim his job, even with a cut in earnings, he could gradually pay the money back. If there was some small-timer standing in the way, he couldn't. If he couldn't start paying down the debt, he'd probably get killed. But then the loanshark would never get his money back. Whereas, if it was the small-timer who was removed from the arithmetic...

He squelched that line of thought before it became downright criminal. He sucked an ice cube for a moment and luckily a more acceptable tack occurred to him. "I was just thinking," he said, "that it would be quite a publicity coup if, let's say, some accommodation could be reached with this other writer and you were able to announce that Harry Forest, long thought dead, had miraculously returned to resume authorship of his much-loved series. Might drive sales to a whole new level, don't you think? Might get you a nice raise and a promotion. Maybe even your own imprint."

"Or might screw up a perfectly good arrangement. Or might get someone hurt."

"Or might save my life. Come on, Emma, we used to be friends. Give me half a chance to work this out. Please. Just tell me the guy's name and how I can find him."

"I really shouldn't."

"We both know that. And we both know that we all do things we shouldn't do sometimes. Spice of life."

She looked down at her unfinished drink. Then she reached for her owlish eyeglasses and put them on again. She spread her hands flat on the table and was halfway up from her chair before she spoke. "You're a bastard, Harry. His name is Evan Briggs and he lives in Key West. You didn't hear it from me."

TWELVE

Apparently Darla was not the only tourist who didn't care to wade into the weedy ocean; the pool at the Flagler House was busy. There was one begoggled and determined person trying to swim laps, but she kept having to weave around people who were just standing there chest-deep, elbows raised like chicken wings, holding plastic cups of pina colada in their hands. The seats at the swim-up bar were mostly taken; refraction through the water made it look like the patrons' torsos didn't quite line up with their asses. On lounges around the perimeter, people were slathering themselves or each other with sunblock. In some cases the rubbing and massaging seemed to meander past the line between skin care and public foreplay. Richie wondered if maybe there were places on Darla's back and shoulders she couldn't reach herself.

They claimed a pair of lounges at a corner of the deep end, stripped down to their bathing suits, and eased into the water. A few people smiled at them, as people tend to do when newcomers enter a swimming pool in tourist places. They smiled back and waded a few steps in no particular direction. Darla said, "I bet they all think we're a couple."

Richie shrugged.

She said, "I mean, what else are they gonna think? Look around. Almost everyone's paired up. Honeymoons. Second honeymoons. Romantic getaways. Must be nice."

"Must be," he agreed, just before he noticed that she was swiveling to face him. She swiveled decisively but slowly, the way things happen in liquid, and very lightly placed her hands around the back of his neck, her fingertips tickling the ends of his damp hair. Their middles didn't quite touch but the lens of water between them warmed and slipped through in a mild eddy.

He was slowly reaching tentative hands toward her waist when a voice rang out from one of the balconies that overlooked the pool. "Darla!"

She let her hands fall. Looking up, she shouted back, "Oh, hi Dad. This is Richie. Another Richie. I picked him up at the beach."

Tony Totes didn't seem too pleased to hear that. Nor, apparently, was he meant to be. Darla flashed him a tauntingly innocent smile.

He shouted down, "Why don't you come upstairs and have a drink with us, honey? We've just finished up for the day."

It was an ambiguous invitation. Maybe Richie was meant to be included, though he had the distinct impression that he was being told to scram. In any case, Darla's answer was clear. "Nah, it's nicer down here. Besides, I'm wet."

After a brief hesitation, her father frowned and yelled back, "Okay, then we'll come down there," and vanished from the balcony.

"Oh great," Darla said softly to Richie. "Chaperones. You see how he acts? He still treats me like a kid. Sees me with a guy, has to interfere. Drives me nuts sometimes."

"Well, listen, if having me here is uncomfortable for you..." Richie began, conveniently leaving out that suddenly running into Evan might get pretty damn uncomfortable for himself as well, especially if Bert was in the mix and trying to keep the whole thing straight in his wise but ancient brain.

"It's not uncomfortable," she interrupted. "Not for me. I'm used to it. It's just the way things are with Pop and me." She scooped up a handful of water and let it slowly trickle down his shoulders and across his chest. "Besides, I'd be very disappointed if you turned out to be the type of person who'd get scared off so easily."

She smiled then gave a decisive kick and swam back toward the deep end before he could come up with an answer.

⚓ ⚓ ⚓

Nacho, his tail whipping around and his breath coming quickly in whimpers of delight, pulled free of his leash and ran straight over to Richie Delinco as the others were stepping through the gate to the tiki bar. The little creature rolled onto its back, kicked its scrawny legs, and presented its belly to be tickled. The display of trust was touching but awkward, since, according to the official story, Richie had never met either Bert or Bert's chihuahua. Darla, watching her companion bend down to play with the adoring dog, said, "Wow, that's amazing. Strange animals always go to you like that?"

Looking up, he said, "Um, not usually. Sometimes."

"Guess they can always tell a good person. Someone genuine."

By then the others had clustered around. Darla made terse introductions. Her father gave Richie a handshake that was well beyond firm and just short of bone-crushing; he stared but didn't smile as he did it. Evan gave Richie a veiled what-the-fuck kind of look as they were presented to each other and pretended to be strangers. When it was Bert's turn, he pulled his wiry eyebrows together and said, "Nice to meet ya. But I thought the other guy was Richie."

"They're both Richies," Darla said. "Funny coincidence, right? Pretty common name, though."

Hoping to drop Bert a hint, Richie said, "If it's easier, you can call me Evan. I go by that sometimes. In my work."

Bert blinked and looked only more confused.

Darla said to Richie, "But you don't look like an Evan. You look like a Richie. Richie's a nice informal name, a name like, I don't know, like a broken-in shirt on the back of a chair. Evan's kind of stiff. Like on a hanger with the buttons buttoned." She gestured toward the other writer. "No offense, but you look like an Evan."

Trying to hold on to his thin smile, Evan said, "Oh, what's in a name? A rose by any other would smell as sweet."

Darla said, "See what I mean? That's something an Evan would say. Lemme guess. Shakespeare again?"

"*Romeo and Juliet.*"

"Oh yeah," said Darla, "I saw the movie. Isn't that the one that ends really badly 'cause the blowhard father won't let the daughter be with the guy she really likes, so she takes poison and everybody dies and the whole audience blames the stupid families with their stupid rules?"

Tony Totes frowned at that, then said, "Just a movie, honey. Made-up story. Why don't we sit, maybe have a bottle of Prosecco."

They moved to a round table under a palapa whose plastic reeds were a pretty good imitation of thatch. When the wine had been poured, Tony raised his glass and said, "Salud! Here's to a good day's work."

After the clink of glasses, there was a lapse in conversation. Richie tried to get things moving. "Darla tells me you're working on a book down here."

Tony said, "Well, that's not really public information."

"Dad, it's a book. You want to sell it or you want to keep it a secret?"

"It's a secret till it's finished. Till Richie here has banged it into shape for me and I can make sure I'm comin' across like I wanna come across."

"And that there's nothin' too incriminatin'," Bert put in, while scratching the dog between the ears. "Or if there is, then ya gotta figure in about the statue a limitations. Which is somethin' that never made a lotta sense to me. A crime is a crime until the clock runs out, then it ain't no more? What is this, justice or a football game? Real life, ya don't see grudges wit' a, whaddyacallit, expiration date. No one sets a time limit on gettin' even. That just ain't human nature."

"Well, be that as it may," Evan said to Tony in what he believed to be an ingratiating tone, "I'll make sure you're totally comfortable with how you're presented."

Richie thought, *Surest way to end up with a really dull and crappy memoir.*

Tony said, "Yeah, I know you will. You're a pro. I can see it." Then he turned to Richie. Hoping for an answer that would belittle the interloper in his daughter's eyes, he said, "And whadda you do?"

Darla spoke up for him. "He's a writer, too."

"Guess anyone can call himself that," her father grumbled.

"And down here a helluva lotta people do," added Bert. "Why not? I mean, it's not like ya gotta sign a whaddyacallit, affidavid. Mailman, ya gotta pass a test at least. Cabbie, ya need a license. Writer, y'order a drink and say that's what ya do. People might come around to thinkin' you're fulla shit, but that's another story."

"He writes fiction," Darla said. Then she looked sideways at Evan. "So much more creative."

"Fiction," muttered Tony, making it sound rather like a dirty word. "Anything I mighta come across?"

"Probably not," said Richie. "I'm sort of, uh, under the radar."

"Under the radar," Tony said. He flashed a vindicated smile at his daughter, as if he'd just proved that this guy she seemed to like was one more nobody she'd picked. "Too bad," he went on. "Maybe someday you'll be on the radar. I'll keep a lookout for your stuff. What name you write under?"

This seemed like a perfectly straightforward question, but by that point there were so many cross-currents that nothing was straightforward. Stalling behind a sip of Prosecco, Richie recalled what he'd already told Darla. Then, slipping an almost apologetic glance across the table at his colleague, he finally said, "Briggs. Evan Briggs. That's my professional name."

Bert fondled the dog. "Easier than everybody's Richie, I guess."

"Evan Briggs," said Darla, tilting her head, letting the name roll around in her mind a moment. "Well, okay, I guess it comes across as more professional, more serious. But I don't know, to me it just doesn't seem to fit. No matter what, to me you'll always be Richie."

THIRTEEN

When the Prosecco was gone and people had got up from the table, Tony discreetly handed three rolled-up hundred-dollar bills to Evan and suggested he take Darla out to dinner, someplace nice. The only problem was that having dinner with her father's ghostwriter was about the last thing Darla wanted to do, so she said she had a stomach ache. No one actually believed this, of course, nor were they meant to. Still, having begged off on spending the evening with Evan, she couldn't very well go gallivanting with Richie, so the little party broke up and people went their separate ways.

It was dusk by then. The breeze had cooled but the afternoon heat still pulsed up from the pavements. Cats made the most of the remaining warmth by curling themselves next to the tires of parked cars. Here and there roosters crowed, no less lusty at dusk than they had been at dawn.

On the quiet walk home to his house by the cemetery, Evan gradually allowed himself to admit that Darla didn't seem to like him much. But why didn't she? It wasn't his personality; he was pretty sure of that. He was pleasant, polite, polished, witty. What was there to object to? He decided that her coolness toward him probably wasn't about him at all. It was simply that Darla was immature, a perverse, contrary adolescent in a grown-up body that she wasn't quite ready for and didn't quite deserve. Major Daddy complex. Lousy attitude. Subversive tendencies. Just plain contrary.

Of course, if at any point she started warming up to him, he reserved the generous option of revising those opinions.

At home on Angela Street, he mixed himself a martini then brought his computer out onto the narrow porch and tried to get to work in the shadow of the looming crypts. He thumbed through his notebook and quickly realized how woefully inadequate his note-taking had been. A scrawl here, a scrawl there; an amputated phrase, a point to pursue that was then forgotten about. It was just bits and pieces, nothing that even remotely suggested the flow and uniqueness of a real voice, and Evan realized with a sudden panic that he'd never before written about an actual human being. Characters, sure, those he could do. Stereotypes, just dial them up. Good guys, bad guys, saintly women, dangerous dames—all the various talking robots of genre fiction who at moments acted or sounded almost as if they were alive. But basically, all they were, were ink blots on a page or pixels on a screen, ciphers tossed together to play a role in a made-up story. But writing an actual person's memoir—this was flesh and blood. Flesh and blood and fear and hope. This was humanity, and it took something beyond mere craft to make it ring true. It took heart.

Sitting there across from the stacked-up graves, watching the light go from coppery to purple, Evan almost let himself wonder if that kind of curious and accepting heart was something he lacked. With a mix of grudging admiration and bitter envy, he almost wondered if it was something Richie had and he did not. He almost wondered if that was why Darla didn't seem to like him.

Then he took a good pull of his drink and got down to the business and the craft, at least, of writing.

🌴 🌴 🌴

Darla was brushing her teeth when Ralphie called. She guessed she was glad to hear from him, but it had been a talk-filled day and she didn't really feel like talking much more. She spat into the sink, picked up the phone, and said a rather tired hello.

"Hello, baby. How's Key West?"

To her surprise, she couldn't help smiling at the sound of his voice—the slight rasp, the neighborhood feel of the accent. Truth was, she just liked the guy. She just wished she could decide how much, and how much of it was because of or in spite of her father, and if she was anywhere near the line between liking and loving or if she'd already crossed it but had chosen not to notice. "Oh, it's fine. Nice and warm."

"As wild and crazy as everybody says? Naked parades? All-night bars?"

"Not in this part of town. And I've barely made it out of the hotel so far."

"Good."

"You jealous, Ralphie?"

"Course I am, you down there looking beautiful in party central. How's your old man?"

"Having the time of his life. Talking about himself from morning till night."

Ralphie came out with a quick admiring laugh. "Yeah, he's got some stories. And what about the writer guy? He as great as people were tellin' your old man he is?"

"Not even close. I don't really get the build-up. Just between us, I think he's kind of a drip."

"So you're not fallin' for 'im, wit' his big vocabulary and all?"

"Please. I think he's a phony."

"Good." There was a strangely bashful pause, then Ralphie went on, "I miss ya somethin' awful, Darla."

He waited a beat for a reply that didn't come, then went on. "How long ya gonna be down there?"

"Don't exactly know. A week? Two weeks. Depends how the interviews go, I guess."

"Wish I could be there."

She said nothing.

"Your old man made it pretty clear I was disinvited. Wants to give us some time to cool off, I guess. 'Cept, guess what, it isn't workin'. Not for me at least. I'm not coolin' down at all. You?"

"Ralphie, I'm sorry but I'm just really tired right now. Big day. New faces. Lots of smiling. Probably got too much sun. I just need to go lie down."

"Sure, baby, sure. I understand. Big day. Rest up. Do what ya gotta do. Just wanted to hear your voice, let ya know I miss ya. You and me, Darla, we're okay, right?"

"Sure, Ralphie. We're okay. Don't worry, we're just fine."

Tony Totes couldn't get to sleep that night. He wasn't quite sure why. Conditions were pretty perfect. There was a light moist breeze blowing off the Florida Straits and through his open balcony doors. A ceiling fan turned slowly and serenely over the bed. He didn't even need the A/C. The soft slap of ocean wavelets blended with faint music filtering up from Duval Street to make a low-key serenade of white noise.

Still, he couldn't quite drift off. Maybe he was too wound up from the hours of talking about his life—the heady mix of relief and invigoration and simmering remorse that went with getting things off his chest. Maybe it was the background buzz of tension with his daughter, the almost constant disagreeing, the utzing back and forth. So he rolled this way and that in the crisp hotel sheets, sampled pillow after pillow.

Then, close to one am, one of his cellphones rang.

It was the private line, the number that very few people had. It hardly ever rang. When it did, it needed answering. He groped toward a switch and turned on a light. He squinted at the phone but the caller information was unfamiliar. He picked up and said, "Yeah?"

"Hello, Tony. How're things?"

"Who the fuck is this and how'd you get this number?"

A low, teasing chuckle came over the line, then a slightly slurring but mellow voice. "I'll answer the second question first. I got the number from you, Tony, decade or so ago, when we were doing business, hanging out. Until I had to leave town for a while. Like, way leave town. For quite a while. Like seven years or so. Sorry I didn't get to say goodbye."

Tony had sat up in bed and was flailing his arms and legs around as he tried to get untangled from the sheet. "You shitting me? Harry? Harry Forest? You alive, you deadbeat cocksucker?"

There was another chuckle, though more wistful this time. "You know, I've spoken to exactly two people since coming back to life, and they've both called me a lot of nasty names."

"Good, 'cause now I'm gonna call you more. You're a cheesy, chickenshit, disloyal, lying scumbag who doesn't even know the first rule of basic decency, which is that you don't bullshit and welsh on your friends. Only a real peckerhead asshole does that."

"Okay, go ahead, Tony, if it makes you feel better, bring it on. I deserve it. I know I do. But the way I stiffed you, look, you don't think it's been on my conscience every day and night for seven years?"

"Bullshit, Harry, you don't have a conscience."

"All right, that was a slight exaggeration. Let's just say I felt bad about it. But I did what I had to do, Tony. My gambling was out of control back then. I wasn't going to be able to pay you back. That's the truth. And I could tell I was running out of time. Your collections guy, Ralphie, like I didn't see the way he looked at me? Once or twice I thought I caught him tailing me home. Paranoid? I don't think so. I figured you were getting ready to have me maimed or whacked."

"Yeah, it was gradually comin' around to that. Not that I was happy about it. Last best option."

"Fair enough. So my best option was bolting and pretending to be dead. Not saying I'm proud of it. But come on, call me all the names you want, how much can you really blame someone for saving his own ass?"

Tony had pulled on a hotel bathrobe and stepped out onto the balcony. Salmon-colored moonlight was tracing out the ripples in the ocean. On the distant reef, a couple of lighthouses were winking. "So what the hell you want from me now, Harry? I'm supposed to tell you I understand, all is forgiven, everything's hunky-dory?"

"Nah, nothing like that. Look, I still owe you three million bucks—"

"Damn straight, you do. Not to mention interest."

"—but I'm hoping maybe there's a way to make things right."

Tony sat down on a lounge and put his feet up. "Would take a lotta doing. But go on, I'm listening."

"I'm planning to get back to work. Take my series back. It still spins off a lot of cash. Enough that I could pay off the debt if you'd give me some time."

"And if you didn't piss away the new cash on bad bets."

"I don't gamble anymore, Tony. Or if I do, it's pocket change. It's under control."

"I've heard that before."

Harry let the comment pass. "But there's a problem with getting my series back."

"A problem. Why am I not surprised? It's always something, some excuse with you, isn't it, Harry?"

A hint of self-pity came into the mellow, slurring voice. "Yeah, I guess it always is."

"So what's the fuckin' problem?"

"I think it's something we shouldn't discuss on the phone."

"No? So what'll ya do, send me an email? Where the hell are you anyway, Harry?"

The low chuckle was back. "According to my phone, I'm in Helsinki. And it might be better for my health if we just leave it at that. Unless I can get a promise from you."

"A promise? That's rich. Like you're in a position t'ask me for a promise or anything else?"

"I'm not. I know I'm not. But I'm asking for a promise anyway. Look, Tony, we both know my word isn't worth shit. Your word is worth a lot. I say that as a compliment."

"Accepted. So what the hell you want?"

"Just your word that you won't ice me if I come to you in person to explain the situation. If that's okay with you, there's a good chance you get your money and I get my career back. If it's not okay, so be it, I guess I'll just keep on being a missing person who can't repay his debts and we'll both be kind of screwed."

Tony thought it over. Based on past experience with Harry Forest, he didn't love the odds of recovering his money even if he played along. Then again, if he didn't go along, his chances were zero. But he had to admit to himself that money was not the only consideration here. In spite of everything, he sort of wanted to see Harry again. The guy had...what? Charm. Charisma. Chutzpah. Presence. Whatever it was that allowed certain people to be real bastards and mostly, not always, not forever, get away with it. He said, "All right, Harry, I'll hear you out. Don't mistake it for forgiveness. But I'll listen."

Striving for a humble tone, the other man said, "Thank you, Tony. So when can we talk? Where can I find you? You in New York?"

"New York? Nah. Right now I'm on, let's call it a workin' vacation. Down in Key West."

Harry almost spilled his nightcap onto his silk pajamas. "Key West, *Florida?*"

"You know of another one?"

"Jesus. Key West. I mean, what are the odds? That's like the luckiest break I've had in years."

"Really? I mean, it's nice down here and all, but I don't see what's so damn lucky about it."

"You'll understand when we talk. Be there just as soon as I can get there. Thanks a million, Tony."

"Three million," said the other man, and hung up.

FOURTEEN

"Jeez," said Bert, "ya put me in a helluva position yesterday."

"Sorry," Richie said. "Wasn't planned. No picnic for me either."

They were having breakfast at Five Brothers Cafe and Grocery on the corner of Southard and Grinnell. Cuban coffee that stained the teeth and left a slightly gritty savor on the tongue that you could taste for hours after. Egg sandwiches on squished-down Cuban bread slathered with butter applied from a paddle.

They sat on a communal bench outside the shop in the shade of the building. The people on their left were bragging about how many iguanas they'd shot in their backyards that week and discussing whether it was better to throw the corpses straight into the trash or stick them in the freezer till garbage day. The people on their right were talking about their outfits for that evening's drag show at La-Te-Da and wondering if sequins and long-sleeves would make them sweat too much beneath their falsies.

"I mean," the old man said, after a slurp of coffee, "*marrone,* it was so confusin' I could hardly see straight. I'm s'posed to call the other guy by your name. I'm s'posed to call you by his name. Him I'm s'posed to be buddies wit'. You I'm not s'posed to know from Adam. Then you come sashayin' in and the stupid dog practically ruins everything by runnin' over to you like you're his best friend inna world. An' this is after the dog totally ignores the other guy altogether except maybe to give 'im a dirty look which, by the way, Nacho has a very effective waya doin', whereby he turns his head way around and looks back across his butt wit' his tail up so his asshole's showin', then lets his eyes close down real slow as if to say *why the hell am I even botherin' wit' you?*"

He paused just long enough to peel back the foil on his sandwich and break off a morsel of glistening bread to feed to the chihuahua in his lap.

"Plus which," he went on, "somethin' else I find confusin' is that Tony Totes seems pretty taken wit' the other guy, which I don't really get, since the other guy is basically just sittin' there wit' his thumb up his ass askin' the occasional dumb question while Tony rambles on. Then again, I guess it's human nature. I mean, we seen it happen, right? Two guys sit around talkin'. Except one guy ain't sayin' hardly anything, and the other guy is goin' on and on wit' his opinions about this, that, and the other, and tellin' stories he's probably told three hundred times. And at the end, the guy who's been runnin' his mouth all day comes away thinkin, *Gee, that other guy is kinda fascinatin'. Can't remember a single goddamn thing he said, but he sure was an innerestin' guy.*"

He broke off for another swig of the thick and bitter coffee. Richie nibbled his sandwich. The iguana people came to a consensus that it was best to put the dead iguanas in the freezer if the garbage pick-up was more than two days away and the temperature was over eighty-five. The drag guys nixed the sequins idea and decided that a generous sprinkling of red and gold sparkles would work almost as well and save a lot in dry cleaning costs.

"But anyway," the old man resumed, "where was I goin' with this? Oh yeah, so Tony seems very taken with his stuffed shirt of a ghostwriter but for some reason it seems obvious he don't like you."

"Well," said Richie, "far as I can tell, he doesn't like me because Darla does, and he doesn't trust his daughter's judgment. I think it bugs him that she found me on her own."

Bert had misplaced his napkin so he absently blotted his buttery fingers on the dog. "Not disagreein'. But let's be fair. Y'also gotta consider first impressions. I mean, what was the guy's first impression of ya? You're standin' there wit' his beautiful daughter by a swimmin' pool ya don't technically belong in, since y'aint a hotel guest. You're soakin' wet, your hair's messed up, your feet are drippin', and you're wearin' a faded rag of a bathin' suit that, if you knew or cared the slightest bit about the finer points a gentlemen's haberdashery, ya woulda given to Salvation Army five years ago. So, no offense, ya looked like a fuckin' bum. Not sayin' that makes ya a bad person. But it didn't exactly highlight your many sterlin' qualities. So let's be realistic. That was Tony's first impression of ya, and first impressions are tough to undo."

"So what do I do?" said Richie. "Get a new bathing suit?"

"Nah, don't bother. Those ratty old trunks have already left a whaddyacallit, illegible impression."

"Indelible?"

"Yeah. Whatever. So forget the bathin' suit. There's gotta be other ways to make Tony see you're not just some knucklehead bum that chats up women onna beach then tags along in a bathin' suit wit' strings hangin' down while she takes ya to a nice pool where really ya got no business bein'. Lemme think."

He rubbed the dog's head. The dog craned its neck and tried reaching backwards with its tongue to lick the last of the butter off its master's fingertips.

"Can't impress 'im wit' a fancy job," the old man mused, "seein' as how y'ain't got a job. Nice new car would help, 'cept ya don't have a car. Big house would do it, on'y ya live in a bungalow, plus ya rent it."

"So you're saying I am a bum," said Richie.

"Not sayin' y'are, just sayin' that from certain points a view, like maybe the point a view of an old-school Papa whose daughter you're chasin' around wit', ya sure as fuck look like one. No offense."

"None taken. Why would I take offense? But then how—"

"How what? How d'ya get Tony to like ya? For starters, ya stay the hell away from his daughter."

"Yeah, but I don't want to do that."

"Understood. Which is why there's no solution to the problem." He shrugged and finally bit into the part of the sandwich that he hadn't already fed to the dog. After a slow chew and a swig of coffee, he went on. "So why not just turn the whole thing upside down and see if maybe there's an edge in it somewhere? Like for instance, the more Darla likes ya, the more Tony's gonna disapprove. But the more Tony disapproves, the more Darla's gonna like ya. Not sayin' it's logical. It's family. Two completely different things. So ya may as well just roll wit' it. Let Tony think you're a crummy guy and a total bum. What other choice ya got?"

FIFTEEN

Harry Forest caught the first flight out of LaGuardia and was installed at Sloppy Joe's by two pm.

It was a slow time at the landmark Duval Street joint. The bartenders were polishing glasses or cutting up limes more than pulling beers or shaking cocktails. The guitar player seemed mainly to be playing to himself, working through songs he hadn't got around to practicing much at home and saving his vocal high notes for later. Harry took one of the red tables on the Greene Street side, away from the music and most of the glare. He hadn't been in Key West in many years, but certain things about Sloppy's, kitchy yet endearing, he remembered: the giant wooden propeller dangling above the bar, the embossed ceiling with vinyl standing in for tin, the college banners hanging limply from the rafters, like life was one big undergrad homecoming weekend. Maybe for some people it was.

He ordered a beer and some fritters and waited for his scheduled meeting with Tony Totes. In the meantime he enjoyed his perch on the cusp between the indoors and the outdoors. On the far side of Sloppy's glassless windows, tourists bustled past licking ice cream cones or twisting their necks to deal with folded but dripping pizza slices. People strutted and ogled each other with a candor they'd never allow themselves at home. Rented scooters rattled past and the dubious narratives of tour guides droned softly in the background. Inside, the light was dim, squandered A/C drifted through the room carrying hungry-making whiffs of fried food, and there was that sweet sense of at least tentative fellowship that pertained in places built on alcohol.

Tony showed up promptly at two-thirty, wearing dress pants and a clean white shirt for the occasion. The two men saw each other from fifty feet away across the mostly empty room. For a long moment, it seemed that both were desperately determined not to smile. Neither could quite pull it off. Rising from his seat and holding out his hand, Harry said, "It's good to see you, Tony."

"And what the hell am I s'posed to say to that, you welshing son of a bitch?"

They shook. They held each other's gazes and each other's forearms. Smiling, the author said, "You're supposed to say, 'It's nice to see you, too, Harry.'"

Putting on a pretended scowl, Tony said, "Well, fuck me, it kind of is. How the hell you been?"

They sat.

Harry said, "Other than dead, not bad. Finland's okay once the sun comes up. No litter. Rich food. Big women."

"Ya marry any?"

"Not a one."

"That's unlike you, Harry. Seven years, no new wife?"

"Sometimes people learn. And you, Tony? New missus? Girlfriend in a cozy midtown nest maybe?"

"Nah, nothin' like that. Not in years and years. I got blindsided once. That was enough."

"Smart. Me, I should've stopped a wife or two sooner. Probably wouldn't be in the fix I'm in right now."

A waiter in a skull-and-crossbones shirt came over to take the new arrival's order. He asked for a Jack Daniels, neat. Harry said he'd have one, too, though he hadn't quite finished his beer.

Tony said, "So this fix you're in..."

"Right. Well, for starters, I kind of outsmarted myself on the alimony thing. No problem with the first four wives. If I was dead I could just stop paying."

"Deadbeat that you are," put in Tony.

"*Mea culpa*. But it's not like I was depriving them of their personal trainers and Hermes scarves and Botox shots. I'm sure they made out fine. Women who marry guys with money go on to marry other guys with money. That's just how it works. Especially if no one's expecting some big, grand love affair."

"You sayin' you didn't love your wives? You used to say you did."

"The truth, Tony? I'm not sure anymore if I loved them or not. And I don't think they loved me much either. Or if they did, they got over it as they got to know me better. But look, let's not make this a therapy session. I used to pay a guy for that."

"Doesn't sound like it helped much."

"It didn't. So I stiffed him on the bill."

The drinks arrived. They were the kind of righteous pours that are the reward for bringing in revenue at off-hours. The two men clinked glasses.

"But anyway," Harry went on, "it was with wife number five that I really got clobbered."

And he told his former friend and bookie the convoluted saga of the vengeful sale of all rights, in perpetuity, to every book he'd ever written.

Tony tried to follow, then said, "So you thought—?"

"I wasn't thinking anything very clearly. I was running for my life, Tony. As you may remember. But the way I thought it would play is that my last wife would keep ownership of the estate and live very comfortably off the royalties, and that if I ever came out of hiding, maybe we could work out some kind of split, maybe even get back together. But there were two things I didn't factor in. Number one, she hated my guts. Number two, she had a girlfriend with whom she wanted to start a whole new life."

"And you didn't know? You didn't suspect?"

"I had no idea. Guess I wasn't paying very good attention."

"Or maybe spreading your attention a little too thin."

"That too. Anyway, so she sold the whole enchilada to the publisher. Even my name. And one thing you should know about publishers. If they own something that's making money for them, they never give it back. So there it is. I'm out in the cold."

Tony listened and slowly rolled whisky over his gums, savoring the burn of it everywhere. Then he said, "Hate to say it, Harry, but it serves ya right."

"I knew you'd be sympathetic."

"To your wives, maybe. But here's the part I don't get. If you've screwed yourself as royally as it sounds like, what's this bullshit about bein' able to pay me back my three mil?"

"I'm getting to that," said Harry, casting a quick but guilty look back across his shoulders and sliding his red chair closer to the table so that it squeaked against the wooden floor. "Want another drink?"

"Nah, I'm good."

"I do." He waggled his glass until he caught the waiter's eye. Then he said, "Well, look, the books still have to get written. Somehow. By someone. So I asked my editor—begged is more like it—if I could have the gig. Just as hired help. At a big cut in pay. It was humiliating. She still said no. They've made a long commitment to someone else. A nobody. A hack."

He broke off as the fresh booze was delivered and treated himself to a long slurp before continuing. "And as long as this hack is on the job, I can't make a nickel."

Tony laid his arms flat on the table. His face was utterly blank. "Yeah? So?"

Harry Forest was not a man who blushed easily, but under Tony's unwavering gaze he now felt the heat rising in his neck and darkening his forehead. His tongue felt thick and he fumbled for words. "So, if this guy, say, were to come around to deciding it was in his best interest—"

"What're you tryin' to say, Harry? Don't be such a fuckin' coward."

"Well, if this guy wasn't in the way..."

Tony's jaw had gradually been tightening down and by now there were hard lumps in his cheeks and hard lines at the outside edges of his eyes. "Harry, listen, I've cut you a lotta slack about a lotta things, but now you're pissin' me off. You askin' me to do a piece of dirty work for you? Do the ugly part while you look away and pretend you got clean hands?"

"No, no. I'm only saying—"

"You don't ask that of a friend. You don't even ask that of your bookie. You ask that of a thug. 'Zat what you think of me, Harry? That I'm a thug? That I take it so lightly to scare someone, hurt someone, get rid of someone maybe? If that's who I was, you'da been dead seven years ago."

Rattled, Harry said, "Look, Tony, I'm not trying to insult you and I'm not just asking as a favor. I'm asking because it's something where we both would benefit. I get my gig back, I can start to repay you."

His eyes still hard, his fingers clenched around his whisky glass, the other man said, "So go ahead, Harry, I'm listening. But talk to me straight and don't kid yourself you're not responsible. Just tell me what the fuck you want."

"Okay. Okay. I think I'd like one more drink. You?"

"No. And you don't either. Stop hiding behind the booze. Just man up and talk to me."

The author sniffed the golden residue at the bottom of his glass then leaned in on his elbows and hunched over the table. "All right. The guy who's writing my books now, he happens to live right here in Key West. I don't know exactly where. I don't know anything else about him. All I know is his name."

"Which is?"

"Evan Briggs."

Tony's eyes widened and his head tilted to the side. "Come again on that?"

Harry said it again.

"Jesus Christ. Small fuckin' world. I've met that guy."

"You have?"

"He's been hangin' around my daughter, which I'm not too thrilled about. She says she met him at the beach. Probably hangs there lookin' for young women he can hit on."

"Sounds like a real lowlife."

"She brought him over to the pool yesterday. His bathing suit looked like somethin' from a dumpster. Embarrassing. Come to think of it, he kind of mentioned he was working on a novel."

Working hard to mask his glee, Harry said, "Well, there you go. He's our guy. And it doesn't sound like you like him too damn much to begin with."

"My daughter tends to pick the strays and losers. I'm always hopin' to find someone better for her. Gotten me nowhere so far."

"Might have a better chance if she wasn't wasting time with this slimeball. Not to mention that he's standing between you and getting your three million dollars back."

"There's that," said Tony. He swirled what remained of his whisky and took a contemplative sip. "Ya know, it's kind of funny how these pieces are fittin' together. I mean, part of the reason I brought Darla down here inna first place was to get her away from Ralphie, who she's been dating. You remember Ralphie, right?"

"Oh yeah," Harry put in. "I remember Ralphie only too well."

"So I'm doin' what I can to split them up, and what happens? In about ten minutes, she's hauled in another guy I don't approve of. Now it turns out there might be business advantages to convincing this new guy to step aside. And if it comes to that, who's gonna be doin' the convincing? Ralphie, who I imagine would be delighted to have the new guy on the sidelines or otherwise out of the picture."

"Sounds like everybody wins," said Harry.

"Not everybody. You know and I know there's no such thing as a game where no one loses."

The author just lifted his eyebrows and shrugged at that. He'd gotten his composure back and he felt pretty sure he'd said enough. He folded his hands in front of him and looked down at his empty drink. Outside, beyond the glassless windows, the tourist train lumbered by, the driver spouting nonsense. Inside, the guitar player strummed a last chord and announced that he'd be taking a short break. No one seemed to care.

Tony finally polished off the last drop of his whisky and almost daintily dabbed his lips on a pocket handkerchief. Then he said, "Don't take me for granted, Harry. Don't take anything for granted. But I'll think it over. I'll give it some thought. Maybe I'll call Ralphie."

PART III

SIXTEEN

"Dad," Darla asked sweetly, "why's Ralphie coming to town?"

"Who said he is?" Tony asked in return.

"Oh, no one."

They were sitting at breakfast—father, daughter, Bert and Nacho. The rolling table had been wheeled onto the terrace and its cloth now held a scattering of muffin crumbs and Rorschach blots of coffee spills. There were picked-over baskets of croissants and rolls and a platter of the underripe melon and fibrous pineapple that are the hallmark and shame of hotel fruit plates everywhere. Low yellow sunshine skidded across the surface of the ocean. The morning's first jet-ski roared up out of nowhere and raised a scar in the water.

"Only," Darla went on after a sip of coffee, "we talked on the phone a little while ago and suddenly he's asking me all these questions about the weather. Which seemed a little strange 'cause Ralphie's not a weather kind of guy. Suddenly he's asking me like how cold does it get at night? Has there been much rain around? You know, things somebody might ask if they were packing for a trip. I asked him what was up. He said just curious. Which usually he isn't."

Tony said, "Sometimes you're too clever for your own damn good, Darla."

"Or maybe Ralphie isn't," Bert put in.

"You weren't supposed to know. At least not for awhile."

Bert said, "Sounds like Ralphie wanted her to know right off the bat. Either that, or Ralphie ain't too bright."

Tony gave a slightly annoyed shrug and tore off a piece of a roll. "Sometimes Ralphie doesn't think before he talks. Or does things. Anyway, it's not a social visit."

"I picked up on that," said Darla. "So why's he coming?"

"You don't need to know. Something's come up. I need him down here. Don't expect to see much of him. He won't be staying with us."

Bert was sawing through a slice of the woody pineapple. He tried to take a bite but it hurt his teeth. He offered it semi-chewed to the dog. The dog didn't want it either. He put the rejected morsel aside and said, "He's gonna be stayin' at my place."

"Which I really appreciate," said Tony.

"No problem. It's a real headache tryin' ta get a short-notice hotel room these days. Or even a whaddyacallit, whatever the heck those initials are. Unbelievable, the way people keep on flockin' down heah. Hurricanes, no hurricanes, anybody care? 'Zere anybody left in Michigan? 'Zere anybody left in Canada? Ohio, maybe there's eight people. They got the fuckin' state to themselves. Cleveland, Cincinnati, anywhere they want they can go. Anyway, I got a couch and an espresso maker. Long as Ralphie's not too picky, no problem for me havin' him stay."

Just then there was a knock on the front door of the suite. Darla got up to answer it.

Evan stood in the doorway, dressed in another shiny shirt from the far back of his closet, flashing the nervous smile that made his lips go flat as anchovies, ready for another day of posing as Richie and listening to Tony Totes tell his rambling stories.

She gave him a rather chilly hello and decided to go out for a walk. Or maybe do a little shopping. She didn't really know what she felt like doing. She only knew she wanted to do it someplace else.

⚓ ⚓ ⚓

Tony and his ghostwriter and Bert and Nacho settled into the white furniture of the living room. Evan had the yellow pad on his knee. Bert had the dog in his lap. After some chitchat, Tony cracked his knuckles and said, "S'okay, you remember the story I told you a couple days ago about the guy I trusted who stiffed me big time?"

"Sure, of course I do. About the writer. Harry Forest." Ingratiating as ever, he added, "It's a terrific story."

"Well, don't write it yet."

"Don't write it? Well, sure, Tony, whatever you say. Although it would set me back a little bit. I was thinking about featuring that story up front, as a sort of prologue, you know, to establish your more human side."

"What other sides he got?" asked Bert.

The question flustered Evan. "Well, you know, the...the business side. The practical side."

"Not to quibble," the old man said while fondling the dog, "but those sides ain't human, too? They're all human. That's the fuckin' problem wit' people. Too many goddamn sides to 'em."

Evan didn't really have a response to that, so he turned to Tony and said, "Well, be that as it may, may I ask why you don't want me to write that story?"

"'Cause maybe it ain't finished yet."

"But it is," said the ghostwriter in a rather professorial tone. "That's the beauty of it. The person who wronged you is dead. Fate, or karma if you will, took care of your revenge, and yet your hands are clean. Death wrote the perfect ending."

"Except what if it didn't?" Tony said.

"Excuse me?"

"What if Harry Forest isn't dead?"

"But he is."

"Let's leave that on the side for now. What if he isn't?"

"But—"

"Then the story wouldn't have an ending yet, would it? It would still be goin' on. There'd be different ways it could go. Why waste time workin' on a story where you think you're at the end but it turns out you're somewhere in the middle?"

During this exchange, Bert and Nacho had been twisting their heads back and forth in perfect sync. With Tony's last question still dangling in the air, the old man said, "'Scuse me, but I'm findin' this hypot'etical or ya might say theoretical discussion a little bit elevated and perplexin', and I don't really see where all this speculatin' and conjecturin' is gettin' us. Seems to me it comes down to a pretty simple question. This Harry guy is dead or he's alive. He can't be bot'."

"Actually," said Evan, "there's a very famous physics experiment about a cat that's both—"

"Which is no doubt very edifyin'," Bert interrupted, "but we ain't here to talk about a half-dead cat. We're here to talk about this Harry guy and what his bein' dead or alive might mean to Tony. And since I'm kinda helpin' out on a pro bono basis, which means I ain't gettin' paid nor would I wish to, just lookin' out for Tony's interests, I got a couple concerns. Basically, it comes back to the rather arbitrary or even whimsical rules about the statue a limitations, which we were discussin' just yesterday or maybe the day before, who the hell remembers? Anyway, if this Harry guy is dead, and been dead for a long time, and Tony wasn't involved or let's say implicated in the unfortunate circumstances that occurred, then we don't have a problem and you can just tell the fuckin' story wit' impunity or immunity or insouciance or however ya like. However, in the extremely unlikely event, which never even struck me as even the remotest possibility until like two minutes ago, that this Harry fella is alive, then it's a totally different can a worms wit' a whole new set a pitfalls and pratfalls or shit that could go wrong. 'Cause now we're inna present, aka now, where the time-clock on the statue a limitations ain't even started windin' down yet, so if somethin' bad or even fatal was to happen to Harry, leavin' aside how richly he deserves it, then it would be day one onna limitations clock and ya might wanna be extra careful about sayin' anything that might suggest that Tony had a motive for wishin' Harry ill, which in turn could turn out to be incriminatin', which of course could make ya regret that ya said it in a public way, like for instance in a book. That's all I'm sayin'."

"Took a long time to say it," Evan couldn't resist observing.

"So what? Ya got a train to catch?"

"Look," the writer pressed. "The man is dead. It's been well-established that he's dead. It's been in *The New York Times*. Why don't we just move forward?"

Bert paused, then turned his face downward and met his chihuahua's glassy gaze. "Nacho," he said, "didn't I just tell the guy exactly and precisely why we shouldn't just move forward? Ya think he wasn't listening?"

"I was listening. Of course I was listening, but..."

"Look, enough," said Tony Totes. The voice was soft but very firm. For the first time during their work together, it sounded unmistakably like a boss's voice that left no room for argument. "Bottom line, I don't want that story written down just yet. Got it?"

Evan nodded but not without a hint of petulance.

"So let's move on," said Tony, easing back in his chair and looking expectantly at his ghostwriter.

Evan sent back only a blank glance.

"Come on, Richie, you're the interviewer. Ask me somethin'."

Evan squirmed. Unpracticed in the delicate art of drawing people out, he could think of nothing to say. Finally, he coughed softly into his hand, then said, "Um, maybe you could explain to me about the vig again."

SEVENTEEN

In the takeout line of the Cuban Coffee Queen on the wharf at Key West Bight, an older man with a handsome though weathered face and a leonine silver mane approached a striking dark-haired woman probably less than half his age. "Excuse me," he said "but I have the feeling we've met before."

It was the lamest and tiredest pickup line in the whole wide world, and it was only good manners that held Darla back from laughing in the old guy's face. Instead, she just flashed him an unsmiling glance and said, "No, I don't think so." Then she turned her attention to the hand-scrawled menu hanging on the wall behind the counter.

A moment later, the old guy at her shoulder tried again. "Wait, it's coming back to me. We have met. It was in the City. Years ago. You weren't much more than a kid. High school maybe. I was with your Dad. It was late. He was picking you up from something. Basketball game, concert, something like that. This sounding familiar at all?"

She swiveled and looked at him more closely, her expression going from bothered to disbelieving. "Mr. Forest?"

"Jeez, I wouldn't have remembered that. Your father made you use last names back then. Very old-school."

"But...But you're supposed to be dead."

He came out with a mirthless little chuckle. "Supposed to be dead. Interesting phrase if you think about it. Supposed to be as in *thought* to be? Or as in *should* be? Well, anyway, now you can call me Harry."

Once she got past the initial shock of seeing him alive, she half-turned away from him and looked down at the floor. "Sorry, but I'm not sure I want to call you anything."

"Oh. So you're mad at me, too? Along with everybody else?"

"Look, I don't really know you and I don't really want to know you. All I know is that you're the guy who let my father down so badly. Disappointed him like no one else. Maybe even broke his heart in a way. Made him lose his faith in people."

Harry's eyebrows sagged. He pressed his lips together and slowly shook his head. "You know, a lot of nasty things have been said to me in the last few days. They've pretty much rolled right off my back. A few I've even taken as sort of screwed-up compliments. But that one hurts."

"Good." She looked over at the menu board again.

He said, "You're very loyal to your Dad."

"Yeah, I am. And he's loyal in return. That's how it's supposed to be, right? Loyalty cuts both ways. Guess no one ever taught you that."

"Listen, um...I'm sorry, I can't remember your first name—"

"It's Darla."

"Listen, Darla, you've probably heard some really lousy things about me, and probably most of them are true. But there just might be a few things that maybe you don't have exactly right or fully understand. Can I buy you a coffee? Do you have a couple of minutes to chat? Maybe we'd both feel a little better if you decided that you didn't have to hate me quite so much."

She crossed her arms and thought it over. In the end, simple curiosity won out and she agreed.

They ordered their *con leches* and brought them from the dimness of the coffee shed out into brilliant sunshine that put spangles of glare on the hulls in the bustling marina. Nimble flats skiffs buzzed here and there, their decks hardly higher than pie-plates on the water. Stately old schooners stood squat and sturdy in their berths next to fast but spindly catamarans being prepped for the afternoon booze cruise. Holding their cardboard cups, the unlikely pair dodged and weaved through the crowds on the boardwalk until they finally found a vacant bench.

After a first sip of the thick and creamy coffee, Harry said, "Darla, look, maybe I can't change how you feel, and maybe you don't even want to hear some of what I have to say. But I want you at least to understand that your Dad and I had a very powerful and complicated friendship. I guess these days it would be called a bromance."

"Sounds like something from a beer commercial."

"Okay, trivialize it if you want—"

"Sorry. I was just being mean. Please go on."

"Well, I think the truth is that your father and I were infatuated with each other."

"Oh Christ, you're not going to tell me that you and Dad—"

"No, no. Nothing like that. Forget about that. Sex gets too damn much emphasis in things. Always grabs the headlines. No, what I'm talking about is a new friendship that has some of the same excitement, the same intrigue, as having a new lover. Meaning you just get a big kick out of each other. You look forward to hanging out. You feel good about yourself being around this person. You have things to learn."

Darla sipped coffee and looked down at her lap.

Harry went on. "Your father's world fascinated me. It was colorful, dangerous, even mythic. And my world seemed to strike him as glamorous and glittering. Way more glamorous and glittering than it seemed to me. But then again, I was used to it. So I guess that's really the whole point. We fed each other's fantasies of what it might be like to lead someone else's life."

"Except you were living yours with someone else's money," Darla put in tartly.

"Okay, score one for you. But that doesn't happen to be exactly accurate. It certainly wasn't that way at the start. Maybe you don't remember, maybe your father conveniently glosses over this part, but he wasn't that much of a bigshot when we started doing business. He was a bright guy on the make, an up-and-comer. And he got plenty of mileage out of having me as a client. I gave him credibility in certain circles. Raised his profile. Vouched for him."

"So I guess he should be grateful that you ran up a huge tab before you bolted."

"No, he should be pissed off, and he is. But listen, Darla, things are always more complicated than they look at first, never black and white. And you can't judge or understand a friendship or a love affair or even a business connection if you only look at how it ended. A lot of things end badly. Most things, probably. That's why they end, right? So something ends and you just write off all the good things that happened along the way? The laughs, the thrills, the things we learned from each other? You pretend they weren't there? You pretend they don't count? You pretend they aren't part of you?"

Darla crumpled up her empty cup and put it on the bench beside her. She looked out at the marina. Pelicans stood unsteadily on pilings, their absurd feet too big for their pedestals, now and then flapping their wings for balance. Gulls bombed in, fighting over scraps. Anchored sloops and yawls swayed lightly on criss-crossing wakes, their masts nodding discreetly at each other as though tipping their hats.

Finally, she said, "You're a good talker, Harry. I'll give you that. My father always said so. Charming. Reasonable. Always knowing the right thing to say. I just wish I could tell if you mean any of it. Do you even know if you mean it anymore?"

He met her eyes and held them. "I mean every word. And I'm not trying to convince you of anything. Why would I? I'm just trying to flesh out the story, remind you there's more than one way to look at it. Maybe it'll help you understand."

She dropped his gaze, pursed her lips, and started to rise.

He went on softly. "The French have a saying, Darla. Maybe you've heard it. To understand all is to forgive all."

Turning to face him, not smiling, she said, "I guess that's swell if you're French but I'm not sure it would wash with Sicilians. Anyway, I'll try not to hate you, Harry, but I'm not sure I can manage it. In the meantime, please do yourself and all of us a favor. Don't disappoint my Dad again. Nothing good could come of it. Thanks for the coffee."

EIGHTEEN

Ralphie's flight was due in around 4 pm, so Bert started getting ready to go to the airport around three. Not that Ralphie needed a personal pickup any more than Tony had. Bert and Ralphie had never even met before. But the enforcer's arrival was an excuse to start up the old Caddy and see if dry rot had finally broken through the flaking white sidewalls. Also, it was another opportunity for him and the dog to dress up. He decided on houndstooth caps this time, along with jerseys stamped with a vintage Corvette motif.

But the main reason Bert wanted some quality time with Ralphie was that, as usual, he was after information. That morning's session at the Flagler House had been tantalizing but puzzling. Suddenly Tony's enforcer was coming to town. Why? Tony hadn't felt like saying, and no matter how many different ways Bert tried to phrase the question, Tony dodged it every time. Of course he did. He was a pro. And on top of that, he'd suddenly started backpedaling about telling the Harry Forest story, which he'd been gushing to tell just a couple days before. What was up with that? Did he have some inside intel that Harry Forest was alive? Was it just some crazy hunch? Some guilt thing about wishing Harry dead? Did he decide the story made him look dumb for getting suckered, or weak for letting it slide so long? And what the hell did it have to do with Ralphie suddenly flying to Key West?

Undaunted after having zero luck squeezing answers out of Tony, Bert thought maybe he could finesse a reveal or two from Ralphie, who by repute was not the fluffiest pillow on the bed. Then again, it was entirely possible that Ralphie didn't know squat about why he'd been summoned. Still, an airport trip was always an occasion, so the old man pulled on his calfskin driving gloves and started searching for his car keys.

⬆ ⬆ ⬆

In the yellow cottage at the clothing optional compound, Richie Delinco, tapping away at the computer in front of the louvered window, was having what felt to him like a breakthrough day. He was discovering that things went better if he didn't try quite so hard to tell the story. If he relaxed his posture and his attitude, if he unclenched his fingers and let them range along the keyboard, the story would begin to tell itself. All he had to do was stay out of the way and trust it. If he trusted it, so would readers. He didn't need to put words into characters' mouths. He just needed to listen when they talked, to allow himself to be surprised by what they said. It wasn't his place to invent emotions for them. Their emotions were their own; he only needed to feel what they were feeling. He didn't need to be a judge of right and wrong or a referee of arguments. His job was both more humble and more mysterious—more like being the midwife of a story determined to be born.

So he felt loose and invigorated and the pages were piling up and the scenes were ringing true.

That's when Evan called.

His voice was choppy and rather breathless. He said that something very weird had happened and they needed to talk right away and could he please stop by on his way home from the Flagler House.

Richie looked at the half-finished sentence on his computer screen. "How about we get together later? I'm kind of on a roll right now."

"I don't think this can wait," Evan said jumpily. "I mean, it's weird. It's Kafkaesque."

"I hope you're not throwing that literary crap around with Tony Totes."

"Only when appropriate. Got any gin at your place?"

"Sorry. Just wine."

"Shit. I'll manage. What's the address?"

Feeling his momentum scraping to a halt, Richie passed it along.

Ten minutes later Evan stepped through the compound gate and into the courtyard, where a number of residents were arrayed on poolside lounges, sunning themselves in a manner that would leave no tan lines. They glanced up at the new arrival as though he were a visitor from another country, another world; someone with pants on, long pants, and a shiny long-sleeve shirt with sweat marks on it, and real shoes meant for walking on pavement, with socks no less; an apparition. Evan, in turn, blinked down at the part-time nudists, some of whom had pebbled dents in their asses corresponding to the slats of the lounges. Two large pierced women were moving synchronously in the pool—aerobics? Zumba? Sufi dancing?—and the water they displaced was splashing onto the apron in small tsunamis.

Richie waved from the doorway of his bungalow.

"Interesting place," said Evan as he tiptoed over, avoiding the puddles. "Must be a little distracting."

"At first. Not anymore"

"Probably gets a little rowdy sometimes."

"Compared to what? The cemetery? Life makes noise. So what's the big news that couldn't wait?"

"How about that glass of wine you promised me?"

They moved into the dim, cool living room. Evan sat down on a lumpy sofa whose faded upholstery bore a grandmotherish floral pattern and gave off a faint nostalgic whiff of mingled mildew and moth balls. Richie went to the kitchen and poured out two glasses of Sauv blanc. When he came back to deliver one to his colleague, he noticed that Evan was having the damnedest time keeping his legs still.

"You getting manic again?" he asked.

"Manic. Nervous. Panicked. Why stick a label on it? Cheers." He took a gulp of wine and went on. "I just don't like the way this is going and I don't like feeling that I suck at your job. I freeze up when I'm over there. I don't know what to ask. The daughter doesn't like me. Your buddy Bert gets under my skin. Even the fucking dog has attitude. And now this crazy new wrinkle comes up."

Richie eased down into a scuffed wicker chair and put his drink on a small table with a cracked glass top. "So what's the wrinkle?"

Evan crossed and uncrossed his legs. His fingertips fretted the piping on the seat cushion. "Tony told me this great story and now he doesn't want me using it."

"Happens," Richie said. "Gotta roll with it."

"But you don't understand. I was going to build the whole character around that story."

"Fine, except Tony Totes isn't a character. He's a person. There's a difference. People are allowed to change their minds. So ask him for some other stories."

Increasingly flustered and twitchy, Evan blurted out, "But this story was about Harry Forest."

This puzzled Richie. "Harry Forest? What the hell does Harry Forest have to do with it?"

"Tony was his bookie."

"Jesus. Small world."

"Too freakin' small sometimes," said Evan. "So here's the backstory. Years ago, they get to be friends. Close friends. Harry's gambling spins out of control and he runs up a huge tab. Out of friendship, Tony cuts him more slack and is the last to figure out he's being used. Finally, even though it tears him up to do it, he decides Harry has to go...Anyway, it's a good story, right? The unlikely friendship, the betrayal, the anguish that Tony must've gone through as he slowly realizes he's being duped. It's resonant, right? It's poignant."

"So why won't Tony let you tell it?"

Evan gave an operatic sigh accompanied by a slapping of the sofa cushions. "Here's where it gets Kafkaesque—"

"Don't start with the Kafka shit again, okay?"

Ignoring the comment, Evan said, "So, suddenly, this morning, Tony tells me not to write the story because it doesn't yet have an ending if Harry is alive."

"But Harry's dead."

"That's what I thought, too. Now I'm not so sure. Why else would Tony change his tune? And if Harry Forest is alive, think of what that means."

"For who?"

"Whom," Evan corrected.

"Fuck you. Whom then?"

"Well, for starters, for me. I'd probably be out of a job. The real Harry Forest comes back, you think the publisher still wants me?"

"They're getting you cheap. And I seem to remember you have a nice long contract."

"Which I'm violating every day, thanks to your crackpot idea—"

"That I was happy to let go of and you shamed me into sticking with—"

"And if anybody finds out what we're doing, they'll void my deal in a New York second."

Richie sipped some wine and said blithely, "All the more reason we can't let anyone find out. You just need to roll with the changes."

The other man squirmed and his pulsing eyes panned appraisingly around the funky bungalow. "Nice that you can be so fucking calm about it, renting this annex to a low-end nudist colony. I have a house. I have a mortgage."

"And I have a novel to write," said Richie as he started rising from the wicker chair, "which I'm actually starting to enjoy."

"You're enjoying it? You bastard!"

"It's kind of fun. No one tells me what I should or shouldn't say."

"Shit. I wish I had my old job back."

Richie just turned his palms upwards and gave his shoulders a lift. After a brief pause, he said, "But hey, something just occurred to me. Not that the whole business isn't all about you. But if it happens to turn out that Harry is alive, what does it mean to Harry?"

"I guess it means he isn't dead."

"For the moment. But what then? Does Tony follow through and have him killed this time around? Does Harry end up dead again? What would that do to your poignant little story?"

NINETEEN

In Bert's expert opinion, Ralphie ticked most but not all the boxes for a classic knee-breaker. He had the physique for it, for sure. A solid six-feet tall, maybe pushing six-one. Big shoulders suspended from his neck by ropy strands of muscle. Thick arms whose outline stretched his shirtsleeves, and big hands whose prominent knuckles looked hard as the bones in a porterhouse.

But the mouth and eyes left some room for doubt. They seemed a bit lacking in cruelty, in the unflagging meanness and unquenchable anger that, for some guys, made the enforcer's job a sadistic pleasure rather than a messy chore or guilt-ridden torment. All in all, Ralphie looked like someone who could definitely hurt you but might possibly feel bad while he did it. His big brown eyes might be apologizing even as his fists did damage. Then again, you could never tell in advance what a guy's hot buttons were, what kind of things would make him truly angry and instantly transform his seeming mildness into the sickly joyful frenzy of administering a first-rate beating. If Ralphie had that simmering rage inside himself, he masked it better than most.

That, at least, was Bert's first impression as the two men shook hands and Ralphie folded his big body into the El Dorado at the airport. As the ancient car pulled slowly but loudly away from the curb, the younger man said, "Jeez, Bert, it's so nice a ya to pick me up, put me up."

"No problem. Just want ya to feel like you're wit' friends and family. Relaxed. At ease. No need for secrets, ya know what I mean."

"Yeah. Sure. Thanks."

Nacho, meanwhile, had made the leap from the driver's bucket seat to the passenger's and was giving Ralphie a good sniffing. Then he sneezed.

"Dog's allergic to cologne," Bert said. "'Specially the sweet ones."

"Ah, sorry."

"Not your fault. I mean, he likes it. He's drawn to it on people. Curious, like. Then it makes 'im sneeze. Ev'ry fuckin' time. Ya'd think he'd have it figured out by now. Dumb dog."

"Usually I don't wear much," Ralphie confided. "But today, ya know, the travel, the sweatin'."

"Yeah, I get it."

They turned onto A1A. In the late afternoon sun, the green ocean gave off a muted shimmer like the dull side of aluminum foil. Matted seaweed undulated near the shoreline.

Ralphie said, "Darla doesn't like it either if I splash it on too heavy. Usually it's just a little dab after a shave. Ya know, get that little tingle, close up the nicks."

"Yeah, I get it," Bert said again. Then, sensing a possible opening to ferret out some information, and not minding being a bit disingenuous when the situation called for it, he said, "So that's what brings you down here? Seein' Darla?"

"Don't I wish. Maybe I'll get to see her a little bit. Hopefully find out she ain't seein' someone else, at least. But it's a business trip."

Bert was hoping for more, but the big man clammed up and looked out the window. Chatting about cologne use was one thing, discussing professional matters apparently quite another.

Thwarted for the moment, Bert just drove on very slowly with Nacho in his lap. A line of cars, rented red convertibles mostly, soon built up behind him. Someone honked his horn. Bert ignored it. Nacho barked. The pace felt somewhere between a funeral procession and a parade that nobody showed up to watch.

Eventually, worn down by the tempo and the silence, Ralphie spoke again. "I don't think Tony's too crazy about me and Darla hangin' out together. I mean, he's never come right out and said don't do it. And 'course he can't tell Darla not to, not any more than I can tell her to cut out flirtin' wit' other guys, even though it makes me crazy jealous sometimes, 'cause Darla's one a those people, ya tell her somethin' and it just makes her wanna do the opposite, which is how she is and parta why I like her. But anyway, Tony don't make it easy for us to spend time."

Bert said, "But he brought you down here where she is."

"Yeah, that's true."

"So I'm guessin' the business must be pretty important."

Ralphie shrugged and kept looking out the window. A salt marsh and a time-share joint slid by in super slo-mo.

"An' I don't think he's been takin' bets or makin' loans down heah," continued Bert. "So prob'ly it's somethin' from before. Somethin' that's been hangin' over 'im, maybe. Maybe even somethin' Tony thought was settled a long time ago."

Ralphie said nothing.

Feeling his way, Bert ventured on. "Maybe even something he thought was totally finished."

Without bringing his gaze back inside the car, Ralphie said, "Maybe I thought it was finished, too."

Encouraged, Bert said, "Crazy, ain' it? Ya think somethin's finished. Like, finished as finished ever gets. I.e, dead. Can't get any more finished than dead, right? An' even then ya get fuckin' surprises."

"Big surprises sometimes," Ralphie offered.

The rumbling Caddy reached the driveway of the Paradiso Condominiums. Bert drove right past it. He was finally making some headway with the laconic enforcer. He wasn't going to cut the ride short now. He just needed to pick a place to drive to. So he hung a right on Bertha Street, another on Flagler, and headed north toward Cow Key Channel.

"Yeah, fuckin' death," the old man mused while serenely stroking the chihuahua. "I think about it now and then. My age, who wouldn't? Sometimes I wonder if it's like a Buick gettin' pushed off a bridge."

Ralphie said, "Huh?"

"I saw that happen once. Long time ago. Two guys pushin' a Buick off a bridge. I'll show ya the place. Kinda strange."

Ralphie didn't particularly want a tour. "'Zit far? I woulda peed at the airport."

"Nah, just a mile or two up. We can chat as we go. Get ta know each other a little bit. The place, it's innerestin'. So close to town but so deserted. Some rich guy owned a tiny island. Was gonna build his dream house. Needed a bridge. Gets it half built and runs outa money. Ends up in jail for taxes or some shit. That's life, right? Halfway to a dream."

They soon pulled off the highway and Bert picked his way through a sparse, sandy, and rundown neighborhood. Where the road gave out, there was a swath of gray-green scrub and scabby trees and grasping vines; a couple of hundred yards beyond it, half-hidden in the creeping foliage, were the rotted pilings of a bridge to nowhere. What was left of the roadway just stuck out like a bizarre and futile diving board over a swiftly running channel where barracuda lurked, waiting for prey to be swept down-current toward their jaws. Bert stopped the Caddy and pointed.

"So there it is, through that piece a jungle. But where was I goin' wit' this? Oh yeah, death and the Buick. So these guys are pushin' this Buick—"

"Why?" asked Ralphie.

"Who remembers? Sure they had their reasons. Anyway, they're pushin' the Buick toward where there ain't no more bridge, huffin' and puffin' till they work up some momentum, then it starts to go over, one tire at a time, and it starts to tip, then it's in mid-air, then the fender hits the water, then the front wheels, then the back wheels, then there's a big splash that spreads out around a Buick-shaped hole inna Gulf. Then the hole closes up. And that's it. Whole thing took about ten seconds...So my point is...What's my point? Oh yeah. Person dies, what happens? Just a person-shaped hole inna world that right away fills in again? Yes and no. Not really. I mean, it's a helluva lot more complicated than sinkin' a Buick. People have friends, family, obligations. Those holes don't fill in so easy. Then again, I guess you could also say that people have slots. Jobs, whatever, stuff like that. Like even wit' the Buick—"

"We're back to the Buick?"

Bert ignored the interruption and started driving back toward town. "Say it had a parkin' space—a slot. Slot don't disappear just 'cause the Buick did. Slot's still there. Available. Maybe it sits empty for awhile, but sooner or later someone grabs it 'cause usually there ain't enough slots for everyone who wants one. Ya know what it reminds me of?"

"I have no idea," Ralphie admitted.

"That kids' game. What the hell's it called? There's music. There's chairs..."

"Musical chairs?"

"Yeah, that's it. Which, if ya think about it, is a really shitty game for kids. The music stops, you're supposed to dive into a chair and shove the other kid away or trip 'im up or knock him on his ass as the case may be. Useful preparation for later life, I guess, but kinda brutal, let's face it. Anyway, comin' back to this dead guy—"

"What dead guy?" Ralphie asked.

Bert moved Nacho from his lap to the console as he swung the Caddy onto US 1. "The guy you and Tony thought was dead but then gave ya a big surprise."

"I never said that, Bert. I never said that at all."

"Not in so many words, which shows a right and fittin' discretion on your part. But say the surprise was that maybe he wasn't dead after all, 'cause what other kinda surprise could a dead guy give ya, since parta bein' dead is that your surprises are pretty much used up?"

The dog jumped back into his lap. He put it on the console and kept on talking.

"Anyway, what if he shows up alive and his seat is taken, if you happen to prefer the musical chairs waya describin' it, though you could also go back to the slot idea or even the parkin' space, 'cause there's a lotta different ways to describe things and sometimes I get goin' and kinda mix 'em all together. The point's the same no matter what. Maybe the guy's slot ain't there no more."

"I never said that either," protested Ralphie. "You're the one talkin' slots and chairs and parkin' spaces."

"An' I respect your tact. But ya know who is here? You. And it ain't mainly to visit wit' your sweetheart, as you have, not wit'out a certain wistfulness, acknowledged. So what I can't help wonderin' is whether your unexpected presence in our lovely town is somethin' to do wit' this presumptive Lazarus-like person wantin' his slot back."

"I don't know no one named Lazarus."

They crossed the Cow Key Channel, almost back to where they'd started.

"Okay, leave that onna side for now. It's just that, ya know, as an old frienda Tony's, I'd be happy to contribute whatever modest help I might be able to provide in resolvin' the situation, such as helpin' to make sure that everyone, dead or alive, ends up on his proper perch, which I guess would move things away from the musical chairs or Buick idea and more toward a bird type scenario. But you get the drift."

"Sure. I get the drift. Buicks. Chairs. Birds. Thanks. I'll pass it on to Tony. Guess it's up to him who needs knockin' off his perch."

"As is right and fittin'," said Bert, giving his passenger a collegial pat on the knee as they looped past the airport once again. Smiling pleasantly, he switched on the radio for the home stretch. It was an Oldies channel. Oldies were relative. These were quite old, mostly four guys singing on a stoop. Bert hummed along softly if not quite on pitch with the familiar tunes and sped up a tiny bit. A salty breeze filtered through the porous convertible top. The dog had sneaked back into his lap and gone to sleep.

TWENTY

When Darla got back to the hotel, hot and a bit sunburned from her wanderings around town and still shaken up from her encounter with Harry Forest, she found her father sitting in a lounge on the balcony, reading the book that for days had sat untouched on the end table in the living room. As far as she could remember, she'd never seen her father read a book before. The newspaper, the Racing Form, the tip-sheets coming out of Vegas, sure. But a book?

Responding to her curious look, he lifted the volume and showed her the cover. *"Bad Egg,"* he said. "One of the other ones my guy Richie did, that got him recommended. Finally got around to starting it. Really pretty good. Believable. Some laughs here and there. People talk like people really talk. I hope mine turns out that good. Ya might wanna have a look sometime."

His daughter gave a noncommittal nod. She had other things on her mind. Plopping into a lounge across from him, she said, "I just ran into an old friend of yours."

"Oh? Who?"

"Come on, Dad, let's not play games. You know who. Harry Forest."

Tony put the book on a small table next to him. "Ah. I was kinda hoping that wouldn't happen. Small town, though. Guess I shoulda figured. Pretty shocking that he's back."

"Ya think? We had coffee. Kind of interesting. He made it sound like you two used to be head over heels in love."

Tony half-smiled and gave his head a slow shake. "That'd be Harry. Always exaggeratin'. Always over-dramatizin'."

"But is it true?" his daughter asked.

Her father didn't dodge the question but he didn't quite have an answer either. "True? Not true? I don't know, Darla. We were good pals for a while. But love? Ya start throwin' that word around, ya don't get a yes or a no. Ya get a lotta buts and a lotta maybes and a buncha stuff that doesn't quite add up. Harry used to say he loved his wives. So why didn't any of 'em work out? I loved your mother. I thought she loved me. I knew she loved you. So why did she walk out on us? If there was love, why wasn't she happy? If she wasn't happy, could more love, different love have fixed it? After all this time, I still don't understand how love plays into things or doesn't."

He paused and gazed down across the pool to the Atlantic. Cloud shadows unfurled along its surface then vanished on the next puff of breeze.

"As for me and Harry," he went on, "call it friendship, call it buddy-love, what the hell's the difference? Call it two guys hangin' out and drinkin' together as a waya hidin' out from women 'cause we both had lousy track records."

Darla said, "I told him he kind of broke your heart."

"No, your mother broke my heart. Harry did some damage to what was left of it. Long time ago."

"When you had more faith in people," his daughter said.

"Well, don't kid yourself I ever had that much. I mean, look at the business I'm in. Look at who I deal with. Some good people, sure, but not exactly a buncha saints. There's always liars. There's always takers. That's why ya need friends. They're like a separate category, in a different room. Someone from outside the room disappoints ya, lets ya down, it's no big deal, it's kinda what y'expect. Someone inside the room does it, it hurts. That's just how it is."

"I'm sorry," Darla said.

Her father reached across the space between their lounges and touched the back of her hand. "That's nice of ya, honey. Thank you."

A moment passed. Splashing sounds floated up from the pool. Beyond it, over the ocean, an osprey soared and swooped then labored upwards from the shallows with a thrashing minnow in its talons.

Softly, Darla said, "Dad, why's he here?"

"Hmm?"

"Harry. Why's he in Key West?"

"I'd rather not go into it."

"And all of a sudden Ralphie's coming down."

"Yeah, he is. He's here."

"Why? What's going on?"

"Nothing I wanna talk about."

"Someone going to get hurt?"

"Darla, listen. For your own good—"

"Which you always seem to know more about than I do," she interrupted, a sudden tartness thinning out her voice. But that's how it was with family conversations; a single phrase, the tiniest shift in tone could turn them from sweet to sour. "'Cause you still think I'm just a kid. So you act like—"

"Like what?" Tony interrupted in turn. "Like a father who wants to protect his child. It's natural, Darla. Fathers wanna shield their kids from the shitty parts a life, the ugly things that go wit' makin' money."

"Except I'm only halfway shielded," she protested. "It's not like I don't know that nasty stuff goes on, stuff I'm smart enough not to talk about in public. And now there's something going on right under my nose, with people I know at least a little bit, and—"

"Darla, stop, please," her father said softly. "We're never gonna agree on this, so what's the point of arguing? What's happenin' with Harry, it's just not your business. How it all plays out, you don't need to know. Please don't ask me any more. Okay?"

She turned her eyes away and didn't answer. Tony got up from his lounge, kissed his daughter on the forehead, and went into the suite. Darla picked up the book he'd left behind and started reading.

TWENTY-ONE

An hour later, just before sunset, she called Richie and asked if they could get together for a drink.

In equal parts tickled and baffled by the short-notice invitation and the whisper of urgency in Darla's voice, he fumbled then said, "Well, sure, yeah. When? Where?"

"The sooner the better. Someplace quiet."

He thought it over. "There's this old dive on Simonton. The Eclipse Saloon."

Without hesitation, she said, "Someplace not in public might be better."

"Oh." He didn't know what else to say.

"Your place maybe?"

This caught him off-guard. Sometimes months went by without him entertaining a single guest at his little bungalow. Now it seemed he'd have two visitors in the same day, one of them a beautiful woman. A fraction behind the beat, he said, "Well, sure, fine, great. Only, my place is a little on the funky side."

"I'm okay with funky."

"I mean, people take their clothes off here."

"That's a little fast for me, Richie."

"Sorry, not saying we have to. Just saying other people might."

"Guess that's their business. Got any wine?"

He gave her the address and straightened up the bungalow as best he could. There wasn't much to do or that would make much difference. He plumped the pillows on the faded floral sofa where Evan had been sitting only hours before, checked the bathroom sink for toothpaste drips, squared the light quilt at the foot of his bed. He scavenged through a kitchen cabinet to find two wineglasses that matched and wiped the stubborn smudges from their stems and bowls. Then he went to wait for her at the compound gate.

She arrived just at the moment when the sun had set and the western horizon was yellow with a band of improbable soft green hovering above it and disappearing almost as soon as it was glimpsed. She wore a simple pale blue cotton dress. Her hair was still damp from the shower and it glistened even in the dimming light. He went to shake her hand. She kissed him on the cheek. He asked her how she was. She said ready for a drink.

They walked across the courtyard. At that hour it was deserted except for the pair of hydrophilic women who'd earlier been in the pool but now were blissing out in the jacuzzi, so Richie brought the wine out to a rickety table that flanked the cottage door. They sat in wicker chairs with uneven legs; the chairs rocked a little as they leaned in to clink glasses. "Cheers," said Darla. "How's the writing going?"

"Not too bad right now," said Richie, knocking wood. "I think the story's shaping up. Hope it's working. And if it sucks, it sucks. I mean, it's just a book. What have you been up to?"

She sipped some wine before she answered. "Well, I think I can say I've had a rich, full day. Full of surprises. But this afternoon I've mostly been reading."

"Oh?"

"Pretty interesting memoir that my father's editor gave him. So I picked it up. About a guy named Benny Eggs."

Richie drank some wine and tried not to squirm. "Funny name," he said. Then he gestured upward at the unmoving palms that fringed the compound. "My favorite time of day. The way the breeze drops and the fronds just go to sleep."

Not to be deflected, Darla said, "Ever hear of him?"

"Hmm?"

"Benny Eggs."

"Well, um, maybe. I might've. Not really sure."

"Seems he's one of the guys the other Richie ghostwrote for."

"Ah. More wine?"

She looked down at her glass. "I'm good for now."

He topped up his own.

"Anyway," she went on, "a little while ago, while I was reading, something funny started happening. Thirty, forty pages in, I started noticing that the book didn't sound at all like that other Richie. Not in the least. Not even close."

"Shows he's a pro, I guess."

She ignored that. "I mean, there were no fancy Shakespeare quotes thrown in, no prissy little curlicues like *if you will* or *as it were*. It was just straight talk. No showing off. And I started thinking about who do I know that's a writer but talks that way anyway. Without the bullshit, I mean. So who came to mind? You."

"Me?"

"And then it got stranger. I started hearing the book in your voice. Which by the way felt kind of sexy. Which probably I shouldn't admit. But it was like you were telling me the story. The words you use, the way you say things—"

"Lots of writers sound like that."

"Maybe. I wouldn't know. But I can tell you who doesn't sound like that. That other Richie, who pretty much struck me as a phony right off the bat. He just tries too hard. Puts a cherry on top of everything. It's just too big a stretch from him to Benny Eggs."

She paused for a sip of wine. Across the courtyard, the hot tub jets switched off with a loud click then it suddenly got very quiet.

"So I just have to come right out and ask you, Richie. Tell the truth. Am I imagining things or did you write that book?"

He licked his lips and looked down at his toes. He scratched his neck. Then he scratched his leg. Then he scratched his ear. Then he started to talk but stopped. It was one thing to try to fool the whole wide world; it was quite another to tell a lie to someone you liked and who was sitting right across from you. Finally he said, "Jesus, Darla, no one's supposed to know that."

"Well, no one else does. But why's it such a deep dark secret?"

He leaned in on the shaky chair. "Because Evan and I switched jobs without telling the people who pay us."

Puzzled, she said, "Evan? I thought *your* real name was Evan. That's what you said. Evan is your real name and Richie is kind of a nickname."

"Sorry, that was bullshit. Made it up on the fly. Had to. But I'm Richie. Richie Delinco. He's Evan. Evan Briggs."

She drank, then cocked her head to one side as she tried to sort it all out. The two women climbed out of the hot tub. Their dimpled red butts gleamed softly in the dusk. Wreaths of steam curled up from their shoulders.

Darla said, "Okay, I think I have it. You're Richie. He's not."

"Correct."

"And you switched jobs but didn't tell the publishers."

"They wouldn't have gone for it. Publishers don't like to take chances."

"But you guys apparently do."

"Not really. We'd been drinking."

"Heavily, I'm guessing."

"Pretty much."

The women from the hot tub wrapped themselves in towels with flamingoes printed on them and padded off to a cottage on the far side of the pool.

Darla said, "Think you'll get away with it?"

"Well, I hope so, because if we don't, we'll both get fired, probably blacklisted, and I'm guessing your father will be really pissed for being strung along."

"My father doesn't have to know. I mean, I won't tell him. There's plenty of stuff he won't tell me. Only fair, right?"

She lifted an eyebrow and drank some wine. The streetlamps switched on with a sudden buzz. Their unwholesome orange glow seemed to signal to a million insects that it was feeding time.

"But listen," she went on. "My hunch about your book. That was only the second strangest thing about today."

"There's more?"

"Lots." But before she spoke again, she paused to swat a mosquito that had landed on her forearm, then another that was perched on the knee with the scrape on it. "But the bugs are killing me all of a sudden. Mind if we move inside?"

TWENTY-TWO

Burning through what was left of his money with his usual heedless gusto, Harry Forest was paying top dollar for a penthouse at the Old Pier Inn. The accommodation featured a wraparound terrace with a commanding view of Key West's harbor entrance, where tidal surges slammed into a maze of wakes and shoals, and even big boats rocked and bounced like bathtub toys. Across the harbor, the former dumping ground called Tank Island had been renamed Sunset Key and prettied up into a developer's dream of mini-fiefdoms for the sort of millionaires who wanted the cachet of Key West but not the grunge. Farther out, the endless expanse of the backcountry was dotted here and there by islets so low and featureless that they might have been rugs spread out on the water. When the sky was clear, you could see the curving of the earth.

But Harry and his guests were not mainly focused on the view that evening. For the moment they were focused on the cask-aged rum and smuggled Cuban cigars that the host had provided in the hope of fostering a convivial tone.

The gestures, though, weren't quite working for Ralphie, who kept a skeptical look on his face behind the red ash of his panatela. Not that he had a particular grudge of his own against Harry. His grudge was vicarious, based on loyalty to his boss, but sometimes vicarious grudges were the hardest to let go of; forgiveness was that much more mysterious when the hurt was secondhand. Besides, seven or so years before, Ralphie had been given orders to keep an eye on Harry, get to know his habits and his schedule, learn the routes he traveled, in case it became necessary at any point to shoot him in the head or knock him unconscious, tie him up, and throw him in the river. Once you'd started picturing someone with a bullseye on his forehead, it was a little tough to warm up to him again.

So the big man was dubious as Harry Forest steered the conversation away from the refreshments and the panorama and into the business at hand. "Look," he said, "our problem is really pretty simple. There's only one reason I can't start paying back what I owe. Including interest, by the way. The reason is that some total nobody stepped in and took my job. That nobody gets removed from the equation, everything is fine."

Ralphie said, "So what am I s'posed to do about it? Scare 'im? Hurt 'im? Whack 'im?"

Harry picked a fleck of tobacco off his tongue, then shrugged. "That's your department."

Ralphie turned to Tony and said, "I don't like it."

"Don't like what?" asked his boss.

"I don't like it that this nobody ain't a deadbeat. Harry's the deadbeat. Why punish the other guy? He's just a...what would ya say?...an inconvenience."

"A three million dollar inconvenience," Harry put in. "Not to mention interest."

"Whatever. I just ain't sure it's right to take it out on someone who the only thing he did wrong was bein' an inconvenience. It don't seem fair to me. That's all I'm sayin'."

Harry said, "Oh, come on. We're grown men here. Are we really going to nitpick about what's fair or isn't fair?"

"You think it's a nitpick?" the enforcer said. "Someone gets their head kicked in. Which guy it happens to, whether or not he deserves it, to you that's just a nitpick?"

Harry gave up on arguing with Ralphie and pulled his eyes away. He balanced his cigar on the edge of an ashtray, took a swig of rum, then said, "Tony, I believe Ralphie works for you, and I believe that you and I have come to a firm agreement about how this should be handled. So can we please lose the philosophizing and get this thing resolved?"

Tony pressed his lips together, then put his drink aside and leaned forward with his elbows on his knees. In an almost paternal tone, he said, "Ralphie, I know you don't feel great about this. I don't either. Perfect world, it wouldn't happen. But we're talkin' a helluva lotta money here."

"A lot, a little. Ain't the point. Shouldn't be just about the money."

Tony straightened up, gave his shirt collar a tug, shot a quick frown over at Harry, then said, "Well, actually, it isn't just about the money. There's another part of it. I didn't really wanna tell ya. Didn't wanna make it personal. But this guy, this inconvenience, Evan Briggs his name is...well, I guess y'oughta know. The guy's been messin' around wit' Darla."

The big guy snubbed out his panatela. "What?"

"Far as I can tell, he hit on 'er at the beach. And you know Darla. She's nice. She's...impressionable. Nothin' against you. That's just how she is. And I guess this guy is pretty smooth. So he gets himself invited over to the hotel pool. And I happen to see them there. I mean, it's right under my balcony. And they seem to be gettin' along very well. And they're talkin'. And they're laughin'. And...well, I'll spare ya the details, but he was touchin' 'er. I saw it wit' my own eyes."

"Jesus Christ," said Ralphie. "She tol' me she was hardly gettin' out."

"Sounds like she managed," Harry said.

"Well, she didn't have very far to go," said Tony. "I mean, the beach is right up the street."

"Chances are this creep hangs out there," Harry added. "Waiting for opportunities."

"Son of a bitch!"

"All around nuisance," Harry said.

"So look," said Tony, "it ain't the prettiest situation no matter how ya look at it, but I think we all agree that it's annoyin' as hell, so let's please get down to how we fix it."

Ralphie ground his teeth together, glanced down at his crushed cigar, picked up his rum and had an angry swallow. Wiping his lips on the back of his hand, he said, "Okay. Just fill me in on what I need to know."

TWENTY-THREE

"So, the first biggest surprise of the day," Darla was saying, "is that I was walking around town and ran into an old friend of my father's. A guy that everybody thought was dead."

They'd fled from the no-see-ums and mosquitoes by then and had carried their wine into the living room. Darla had settled into the faded old sofa, whose squishy overstuffed cushions cupped up around her legs. Richie was straddling a wooden chair and resting his arms on the back of it. He'd switched on a lamp that had a three-way bulb but only one way worked, so the light was soft and amber.

He said, "Don't tell me. Harry Forest."

"Wow, how the hell you know that? You know Harry Forest?"

"Not personally, no."

"But you knew he was alive?"

"I'd heard the rumor. Just a few hours ago. From Evan. Who happens to be Harry Forest's ghostwriter."

Taking that in, Darla crossed her arms against her midriff and knitted her eyebrows close together. "Except he isn't. Not right now. Not since you swapped jobs. You're Harry's ghostwriter."

That flustered Richie. "Well," he stammered, "sort of. Not really. I mean, this is just a one-off. It's Evan's gig. He's the one with the contract."

Darla said, "But no one knows that. All anybody knows, or thinks they know, is that your name is Evan Briggs and you're working on a novel, and meanwhile Harry's alive and he owes my father a bunch of money and all of a sudden Ralphie's in town."

The quick segues were a bit much to take in all at once, so Richie focused on the final nugget. "Ralphie's in town? Ralphie, your boyfriend?"

"Ralphie, the guy who works for my father."

"But he's also your boyfriend, right?"

"Boyfriend, not my boyfriend, I wish I could decide. I'm confused as hell." She picked up her wine from a side table, drained it, and waggled the glass. "Got any more?"

He climbed off his chair and went to the kitchen for a fresh bottle. When he came back he saw that she had shifted slightly on the couch and was patting the place next to her. "Wanna sit by me, Richie? I like talking with you."

He poured them both more wine and sat. The fat and yielding sofa cushions sort of squeezed them together but also sort of held them apart, each sunk in their separate nests of feathers and upholstery. They clinked glasses again. After a thoughtful pause, Darla said, "Richie, y'ever been in a relationship where you kind of like the other person, but you know deep down that the other person likes you way more than you like them?"

He considered that a moment with a rueful look on his face. "I've mainly been on the other side of that."

"Ah. I could see where that might suck. But even when you're pretty sure the other person likes you more, I mean, it isn't perfect. Sure, it's flattering and all. Takes some of the pressure off, like you don't have to try too hard, like you won't be brokenhearted if it falls apart. But sometimes maybe you feel a little guilty or empty that you don't care more, feel more. Maybe it makes you a little sad sometimes that it's not more even-steven."

"Even-steven's hard to come by," Richie said.

"I guess. But with Ralphie and me, it's pretty lopsided. At least I think it is. But then sometimes I wonder if I'm kidding myself about that. Flattering myself, protecting myself, whatever. Like if I never heard from him again, I'd shrug it off. Which is weird, 'cause other times, not often, every now and then, I can sort of picture a future with him."

"So you're picturing a future but you don't care if it ends?"

"Look, it's nuts. I know that. And it's not like it's a whole detailed future, just a few basics. Very standard stuff. Like at some point Ralphie asks me to marry him. I surprise myself by getting all emotional about it, like that's what it took to make me realize I care. My father's not thrilled but he comes around. Makes us a nice wedding, helps us get started with a little house, Jersey maybe or out on the Island. Six months later I'm pregnant. My father falls in love with the grandkid and starts looking out for Ralphie more, so life gets easier all around. That's about as much as I can picture."

Richie tried to muster some enthusiasm. "Sounds nice."

"Think so? Sometimes it totally gives me the willies. Like, is that really what I want from the only life I got? A house in the 'burbs ten minutes from where I grew up, married to a guy from the old neighborhood who does bad things for my father? That's as good as it gets?" She drank some wine and burrowed deeper into the sofa cushions. "But hey, I'm sorry. I've been doing all the talking."

"I'm not complaining."

"Lotta guys don't listen when a woman talks. They pretend to, maybe. But they're not really listening."

He shrugged. "Their loss. Me, I like hearing you talk. I like the way your eyes get wider and you tilt your chin when you're thinking. I like the way your lips move when you make the words."

She blushed through the sunburn that wasn't quite yet a tan. "Jeez, Richie, you're making this very difficult for me."

"I am? What?"

"I like you. A lot. Way more than I should. You're nice. You're different. I don't meet guys like you. Maybe I'll never meet a guy like you again."

He didn't know what to say to that so he just kept looking at her. Her blush deepened. His mouth felt dry. A moment passed.

She heard herself say, "I've been fighting it, I really have, but I'd really like to make love with you, Richie."

She said it very softly and it seemed to take them equally by surprise. Neither breathed. They became aware of the rasp of crickets and the whine of cicadas filtering in from the courtyard.

Very slowly, he reached out to touch her hair.

She lightly seized his wrist with her fingertips and moved his hand to the back of the sofa. "But I won't," she said. "I can't. I'd like to, but I'm afraid it just wouldn't feel right. Not with Ralphie so close by. I'm sorry. I don't mean to be a tease. I'm just so confused. Hope you understand."

He licked his lips and nodded. "Sure. I get it."

"Some guys wouldn't."

He just shrugged.

"Makes me like you even more."

He shrugged again.

She said, "Maybe just one kiss, though? Can't be any harm in that. One kiss. But a real one. A good one. Would that be okay?"

She stretched upward from the slump of the cushions and leaned in close to Richie. He sidled across the upholstery to meet her and their separate perches eased down into a single enveloping nest. They kissed. Just once.

But it was quite late by the time the kiss was finished.

TWENTY-FOUR

Sometime after midnight, when Richie was once again alone in the bungalow and feeling very dreamy, his phone rang. He picked it up and heard the usual gruff hello from Bert the Shirt. In response, he said, "Jeez, Bert, pretty late to call. You okay? Everything all right?"

The old man said, "Those would be two separate questions, which I will try t'answer innee order they was asked in. First, am I okay? Comparatively speakin', like, say, comparative wit' Methuselah, yeah, I'm fine, an' I thank you for your concern about my personal well-bein'. Ach'ally, I'm walkin' the dog inna shrubbery downstairs from the condo and he's lookin' at me like what-the-fuck, 'cause I walked him a couple hours ago and he did his business in a perfectly satisfactory manner, which frankly he seemed quite proud'a, and which would usually mean we were finished for the evening and would just sit in fronta television wit' some liver snacks till we fell asleep. But tonight we got a houseguest—"

"Houseguest?"

Bert continued as if he hadn't heard. "So the livin' room is taken and I come downstairs for a little privacy. Which leads me to your second question, namely, is everything all right, which the answer to that one is way more complicated and I ain't got time to go into it right now. But I got a question for ya. Your buddy Evan—"

"He's not my buddy. He's a colleague."

"Whatever. Your buddy Evan, where does he live?"

"Why you wanna know?"

"Richie, I believe I just tol' ya I ain't got time t'explain this shit right now. Where does he live?"

"Over on Angela Street, but—"

"What number on Angela Street?"

"I don't remember the number. The 1100 block, I think. Right across from the cemetery. Opposite some big tall crypts. But why—?"

"Sounds fuckin' depressing," Bert said. "Morbid."

"He seems to like it. Likes looking up at graves when he's standing in the pool."

"T'each his own, I guess. So the pool's inna front?"

"On the side."

"Okay, that's enough to go on."

"Bert, this is making me a little bit uncomfortable. Go on for what?"

"Richie, I'm startin' ta detect a certain pattern heah, which is that I keep tellin' ya this is not the time for explanations, and you keep askin' me t'explain, which is gettin' neither of us nowhere. So suffice it ta say that I am dealin' wit' a certain situation inna best way I can think of at the moment, which may or may not be the best way longer term, which no one hardly ever knows ahead'a time, which I guess is why they call it longer term and why it sometimes leads ta bitter and fruitless regrets about consequences one did not intend, aka unintended consequences. In simple English, I'm tryin' to do you a big fat favor and maybe you'll thank me for it sometime. An' if it blows up in our faces, well, that's life. G'night, Richie."

TWENTY-FIVE

Evan had a strict routine that he followed every morning except when he was too hungover. He'd wake up early, usually to the sound of the graveyard roosters, put up coffee, then, while it was brewing, have a brief plunge in the Dip of Death. The pool water would be cool, almost chilly after the nighttime hours, and it would help him shake the cobwebs loose. He'd drink his first cup poolside while doing a gut check on the state of his mania or panic. The odd part was that, if he felt the mania rising or the panic socking in, he'd have a second cup of coffee, occasionally a third. He knew this wasn't good for him, yet he didn't think of himself as a masochist, more as a seeker of intensity, an ambivalent lover of extremes. Whatever he was feeling at a given moment seemed to feed on itself and make him crave more of it.

This particular morning felt like a two-and-a-half cup sort of day, so he was pretty wired by the time he got around to washing up and dressing. Water droplets flew as he scrubbed his face and the dental floss sang as it snapped between his teeth. The comb zipped through his tidy and obedient hair and gave a pleasant prickle to his scalp. His movements were herky-jerky but precise as he gathered up his pens and notebooks in preparation for another awkward session of coaxing stories out of Tony Totes.

He was nearly ready to head out when there was a knock on the door.

It was too early for the mailman. Maybe a neighbor with a lost cat? Amazon? Jehovah's Witnesses? In his hurried-up state, he didn't pause to think about darker possibilities, so he opened the door.

Instantly he wished he hadn't, wished he'd slowed down or could get a do-over on the previous three seconds. He was suddenly facing a thickly-built man whose chest and shoulders were glutting up most of the doorframe and who wasn't smiling.

"Your name Evan Briggs?" he asked.

It was the simplest of questions but in that compressed and befuddling moment there didn't seem to be a correct answer. Evan licked his lips, said, "Um..." He looked down and then looked up again.

The big man seemed to consider that enough of a confession. He put his hands on Evan's shoulders and pushed him backwards toward the living room. As the two of them stumbled through the small foyer, he hit him with a quick right that landed between the cheekbone and the eyebrow. "That's for takin' Harry's job," he said.

Evan's head snapped back from the impact and he was wobbly on his legs. The big man leaned in close and kneed him in the groin. "An' that's for messin' wit' Darla."

The ghostwriter doubled over. His assailant hit him in the belly with an uppercut that knocked the wind out and he crumpled, wheezing, to the floor. He closed his eyes and lay there in the fetal position, struggling for breath and braced for more punishment.

None came. Instead, when he dared to open his eyes again, he saw the big man squatting close to him. His face was flushed but sad and his eyes regretful. In a low voice, he said, "That last punch was a warning, Evan. Don't make me visit you again. It won't be fun, believe me. Be smart. Just stop doin' what you're doin'. Just get the hell outa everybody's way. So much easier if ya do that."

The big man slowly straightened up but Evan decided it was wisest to stay right where he was, with his cheek against the rug and his lungs gradually refilling by way of short and stinging gasps. He watched in silence as his assailant smoothed his rumpled sleeves and settled his shirt-tails under his belt. As he headed for the door, the big man looked back across his shoulder and said, "Piece of advice, Evan. Just friendly like. Ya might wanna get some ice on that eye asap."

🌴 🌴 🌴

Then Ralphie went out for pancakes.

There was a joint down in Bahama Village where hens and hatchlings scrabbled around through the wood shavings on the ground and there were hammocks slung between palm trees where people could chill while waiting for a table. Darla had suggested they meet there for breakfast. It wasn't exactly the kind of intimate place and occasion that Ralphie would have preferred for a reunion with his girlfriend, but Tony kept him on a pretty short leash when he was on a job, and besides, Darla hadn't exactly been lobbying for them to have more time together. So breakfast it was.

He was balanced precariously on the edge of a hammock when she walked in, wearing a pale green sundress that showed off her semi-tanned shoulders. He rose to meet her but when he tried to turn their casual hug into a passionate embrace and a deep kiss, she lightly pushed him back with the flat of her hand. "Come on, Ralphie. Not in public."

He was slightly surprised and slightly miffed but tried to keep his answer playful. "Not in public? Since when not in public?"

"Oh, I don't know. Since now. I'm hungry."

They scored a table underneath a casuarina tree. The pine needles were soft and yielding underfoot but the sticky cones were hard and sharp even through the soles of Darla's sandals. A server came over, slapped down menus and glasses of water that tasted equally of sulfur and chlorine, and walked away.

Ralphie perused the offerings and said, "Whatcha feel like eatin'?"

"Maybe just toast. Toast and coffee."

"Ya just said you was hungry?"

"I was. I am. But toast is what I feel like."

He shrugged, put his menu aside, and said, "So, you been havin' a nice time down here?"

"Been okay. Lotta sitting around. I get out when I can. Look around, see the town."

"Meetin' people?"

"A little bit, sure. Just, ya know, in passing. It's a friendly place. People goof around."

"Hangin' out wit' anyone?"

The question went unanswered while a different server came over to take their order. He had green hair, a nose ring, and didn't seem to like his job much. He asked Darla what she wanted. She said toast. He grudgingly ran through a list of six different kinds. "Whatever," she said. "I like it cut in triangles."

"Triangles," the server said. "I'll see if the kitchen'll do it."

Then he turned to Ralphie, who just said, "Pancakes." Somehow it sounded like a threat.

"Banana? Walnut?"

"'Zat one thing or two?"

"Either, both. Go wild, live the dream."

"Bot' then," Ralphie said, and handed in the menus.

By then enough time had passed that he felt he was entitled to repeat his question. It came out sounding a bit more insinuating the second time. "So, been hangin' out wit' anyone?"

"I don't really like it when you're jealous, Ralphie."

"An' I don't exactly love it when you flirt wit' guys."

She took a sip of the nasty water. "So I guess that means neither of us likes every single thing the other person does. So what're we gonna do, sit here and argue? A week we don't see each other. Now we sit and argue?"

Ralphie frowned down at a chicken trailing a line of chicks, then brought his eyes back. "Look, I'm sorry, baby. I get upset sometimes. But you're right, makes no sense t'argue. Let's talk about somethin' else."

He didn't seem to have another topic to suggest, so she took the lead. "Seen Harry Forest yet?"

The question took the big man by surprise and he said nothing in return.

"I ran into him," she went on. "Had coffee. This is a small town, Ralphie. Things don't stay secret very long. I know way more than my father thinks I do. Not everything. But I know Harry owes money and there's a problem paying it back. So I'm guessing your job is to fix the problem."

"Listen, baby, you know and I know that I'm not s'posed to talk about—"

"I'm not asking you to. I'm just saying I hope no one gets hurt. No one innocent, at least."

Ralphie squeezed his lips together and flexed the fingers of his right hand. He suddenly realized that they ached from hitting Evan on the bones of his face.

The pancakes and the toast arrived. More chickens ran over tracking the scent of the food. The toast was not cut into triangles. The server asked if everything was okay. They said fine.

Ralphie poured syrup on the pancakes. Darla nibbled toast. Then she said, "Ralphie, there's something I want to ask you. If, say, sometime there was a situation where my father told you to do something and I said that I really, really hoped you wouldn't—if I begged you not to—would you do it anyway?"

He was midway through an enormous forkful of banana-walnut pancakes and it took him a long moment to swallow. Then he swabbed his teeth with his tongue and said, "Jeez, baby, that's a helluva tough question."

"Yeah," she said. "I know it is."

TWENTY-SIX

Evan eased up from his living room floor, gingerly poked at his groin and his ribcage to make sure things were intact, and shambled into the kitchen to get some ice for his eye. The first touch of it against his cheekbone made him wince. Then he felt like his brain was freezing. Then the throbbing started to subside and he called his colleague Richie.

Richie at that moment was sitting on his accustomed outside bench at Five Brothers, having a *con leche* and an egg sandwich with Bert the Shirt and Nacho. He put the foil-wrapped sandwich in his lap, pulled the phone from his pocket, and said, "Hey."

Evan said, "Hey yourself, you son of a bitch. I just got beat up because of you."

"What? What the hell happened?" said Richie, frowning over at his companion and turning up the volume so they both could hear the answer.

"What happened? Some gorilla showed up at my door, asked if my name was Evan Briggs, and punched me in the eye."

Richie felt a moment's confusion followed by a twinge of guilt about revealing where his colleague lived. But before he could speak, Bert had craned his neck and leaned in close to the phone like a guest star on an old-time radio show, and said, "Why'd'ya admit it?"

Evan said, "Who the fuck is this?"

"It's Bert. We're havin' breakfast. Why'd'ya admit it?"

"Admit what?"

"That your name is Evan Briggs."

Exasperated, Evan said, "Well...I didn't admit it. At least I don't think I did. I guess I just didn't deny it fast enough."

Bert said, "Shoulda said your name is Richie. Woulda been the better answer."

"Oh, great. Very helpful. I should have said my name is Richie. Or I could have said my name is Groucho or Harpo or Larry or Curly or Moe. I didn't think of it, okay? I mean, Christ, I've been Evan Briggs my whole life. A gorilla shows up at my door and calls me by name, and I'm supposed to have a clever comeback ready? So it's my fault I got beat up in my own foyer? Can you put Richie back on, please?"

Bert leaned away and Richie said, "Evan, look, I'm sorry—"

"You're sorry. Very comforting. So he hits me in the eye and says it's for taking Harry's job, then he kicks me in the balls and says it's for fooling around with Darla, which I absolutely haven't been, though I can think of someone who maybe has. Then he hits me one more just because he can. And by the way, I'm overdue at the Flagler House to listen to

Tony talk and talk and talk, and what the hell am I supposed to do?"

Richie looked at Bert. Bert looked at Nacho and fed him a corner of his sandwich that held a lacy bit of fried egg white. Then he leaned in toward the phone again and said, "Listen, Evan, I know y'ain't havin' your best day so far—"

"And I'm sure it breaks you up, since you never liked me anyway."

This seemed to take the old man by surprise. "Who says I don't like ya? I got nothin' against ya. I mean, you're a little highfalutin for my taste. Sometimes, okay, ya kinda sound like a guy ya'd love to low-bridge in a bar fight. But hey, no one's perfect. And b'lieve me, I'm tryin' to help heah."

"Yeah, help Richie, maybe."

Bert said, "What's wit' the whaddyacallit, siblin' rivalry or whatever it would be considerin' y'ain't siblin's? Anyway, look, I can well unnerstand that in your current situation wit' the achin' balls and such, it appears to you like I'm playin' favorites. But net-net, as I b'lieve will be revealed, I'm tryin' to help yas bot'. And if ya want my opinion, or even if ya don't, what y'oughta do is get your ass to your appointment wit' Tony and tell him exactly what happened."

"Keep the appointment? Are you crazy? And put myself out there for another beating?"

Bert stroked the dog and said with quiet assurance, "You won't get another beatin'. What happened this mornin' was a one-off."

"The gorilla said it was a warning."

"'Yeah, yeah. They learn that line in tough-guy school. But let's think it through, logical like. Why'd ya get beat up? Ya know what it comes down to? It comes down to a case a mistaken identity."

"That's ridiculous. He called me Evan Briggs. I am Evan Briggs."

"Correct. He mistook you for yourself, which is kind of a weird spin onna whole mistaken identity thing, but crazy shit happens when people start pretendin' to be who they ain't, 'specially if they're not too sure who they are to begin wit'. Anyway, the gorilla mistook you for you, except you ain't really the guy he's mad at. He's mad at the guy who's been, to put it in a genteel manner, spendin' time wit' Darla. Namely Richie. And who's Tony's mad at? The guy who's writin' books for Harry. Which he believes, albeit erroneously, which is to say he don't got it right, is also Richie. So, bottom line, just to keep it nice and simple, the gorilla, whose name is Ralphie and who happens to be my houseguest, beat up the wrong guy, which, excuse me, I kinda thought might happen when I set the whole thing up, and—"

"Set the whole thing up? You sent him over here, you antediluvian fuck?"

"Now, come on, let's not get ageist about it. Look, ya got hit a coupla times. Regrettable. But try ta look beyond your little aches and pains and see the bigger picture. Tony still thinks you're Richie, the guy who's writin 'his memoir for him, and he don't want nothin 'bad to happen to that guy, namely you. So you're safe. For the moment. Plus Tony's gonna be very pissed at Ralphie for knockin' ya around, and he'll give him hell, and Ralphie'll be embarrassed and ticked off and start lookin' for someone else to blame, and they'll be all bollixed up about what their next move oughta be, and that'll buy us some time to sorta sort things out. So this is why ya gotta keep your appointment and tell Tony what happened and act like ya have no fuckin' idea why, so then it's his problem to figure it out. Ya see, when ya take a logical approach to how it's gonna play, it's really pretty simple."

There was a brief silence on the line. Richie had a quick bite of his sandwich, which had gotten cold and rubbery. Bert had a swig of coffee. Nacho did a pirouette in his master's lap.

Evan, sounding slightly dazed, said, "Richie, you still there?"

"Yeah, I'm here."

"Good. What the old man just said. That whole rambling mess. Can you please put it into English?"

"Sure. He said you should go see Tony and we'll go from there."

"That's it? That's all he said? All those words, and that's what he said?"

"Pretty much."

"Loses something in translation, don't it?"

"Doesn't it," corrected Richie. "Good luck with the interview."

TWENTY-SEVEN

A few hours later, Ralphie rang the doorbell of Bert's condo at the Paradiso.

Bert was wearing an apron at the time. It had a yellow background and a cheery pattern of bright red tomatoes and bright green basil leaves that seemed to be gently floating through space at many different angles. The apron had belonged to Bert's late wife, and he still put it on every day while preparing Nacho's dinner, as this could sometimes be a messy process. The water needed to be brought to a perfect temperature before being added to the kibble, then mixed together without too much sloshing or splashing. Then the chicken-and-rice loaf needed to be sliced and diced without letting any morsels slide off the cutting board and onto the floor, because if they did, Nacho's paws would start skidding all over the linoleum as he scampered around to lick them up and he could easily get tangled underfoot. Next, the full bowl needed to be lowered smoothly to the floor without any shakes or tremors that might spill the contents onto Bert's slippers. Finally, and not the least hard part, the old man needed to stand up straight up again. Usually the dog was finished eating by the time he managed it. This gave the whole business a touch of the surreal; looking down at the licked-clean bowl, Bert would have occasional moments of uncertainty as to whether he'd actually fed the dog or not.

In any case, there was a longish delay in opening the door for his guest.

But once the door was opened, it took no time at all to see that Ralphie was in a vile mood. His jaw was clenched. The skin at his temples was etched with narrow grooves. His neck and shoulders were straining against his shirt as though trying to shred it seam by seam.

Genial as always, Bert smiled and said, "Welcome back. How's your day goin'?"

"Shitty," said the big man as he stepped across the threshold. "Really shitty."

"Jeez, sorry ta hear it. Ya look like maybe ya could use a drink. Drink and a talk, maybe? Want somethin'? Some anisette, maybe?"

"Sure, Bert. Whatever ya got. Thanks."

Ralphie stepped into the living room. Bert peeled off into the kitchen to grab some glasses and the bottle. On the way back he realized he might look more dignified without the basil-and-tomato apron, so he slipped it over his head and put it on its peg.

In the living room, Nacho was snarling and Ralphie didn't know why.

"Don't mind the dog," Bert said. "He won't bite ya. He's just a little upset that you're sittin' inna chair I usually sit in."

Ralphie started getting up.

"Nah, don't worry about it. Dog's gotta learn he ain't the king a Sheba. Not gonna get his own way every time."

Nacho kept snarling. Ralphie took a different chair.

"Okay, guess he is the king," Bert said. He poured two glasses of the sticky liqueur, handed one to his guest, and settled into his usual seat. "Salud. So, wanna talk?"

Ralphie took a gulp before he tried. "Shit," he said, "I don't even know where to start. It's just one a those days when everything ya do is wrong even when ya think you're doin' good. Like, wit' my little job this mornin'. I thought I did what I was s'posed to do. I sent a message. Didn't hurt the guy too bad. Thought I did good."

Innocently, Bert said, "So what's the problem?"

Ralphie held up a hand and took another swig before he answered. "I'll get to that. But anyway, so then I take Darla out to breakfast. And she treats me cold. Not like she's mad at me. Just...cold. An' I have no idea why, and it's makin' me feel lousy. Then she starts askin' me weird questions. Would I do this? Would I do that? What if Tony told me to do somethin' and she asked me pretty please not to? I mean, stuff we never talked about before. And how the hell do I know what I'm gonna do or not do till I'm inna situation? So I'm kinda buffaloed. Then breakfast is over, she says she's gotta go, and we have this cold hug where she's leanin' back away from me like God forbid we rub together a little bit, and I'm wonderin' what the hell is goin' on."

Bert reached down and lifted Nacho onto his lap. Scratching him between the ears, he said, "Tough ta know where ya stan' wit' people sometimes. Wit' a dog, never. Pure consistency, ya can't beat a dog. Not that he don't have his pissy moods, don't get me wrong. But, like, two percent a how much people do. Okay, maybe five. Bad day, maybe ten."

Ralphie didn't seem to find the dog mood statistics all that interesting. He held out his glass for more anisette. His host poured.

"So anyways," the big man said, "I go for a long walk. Ya know, think things through, clear my head. An' the pieces start to fall together. Darla's treatin' me cold. She's askin' me if I'd hold back from doin' what I'm told to do. An' I start thinkin' why? Prob'ly it's about this guy she's been hangin' wit', this Evan Briggs. Maybe she really likes him. Maybe he's got her really charmed. Which pisses me off and makes me wish I gave 'im a much worse beatin' than I did.

"So I'm stewin' over this," Ralphie went on. "I've walked all over town, an hour, two hours, then I get a really ticked off phone call from Tony tellin' me to get my ass over to his hotel, pronto. So I go. I ring the bell. He opens the door and slaps me."

"Slaps ya?"

"Backhand. Right across the kisser. I could feel his rings. Ever been slapped, Bert?"

Without hesitation, the old man said, "Once. Seventy, eighty years ago. I remember like it was yesterday. Not the pain. The embarrassment. The whaddyacallit, humiliation."

"Yeah, that's it exact," said Ralphie. "He's your boss. Ya can't hit back. Ya just take it. Drives ya nuts, right? Anyway, he yanks me into the place and starts reamin' me a new asshole. Calls me ev'ry name inna book. I'm a fuckup. I'm stupid. Meantime, I got no idea what the problem is. Finally I say, 'Tony, what's the beef? You told me to rough up Evan Briggs, I roughed up Evan Briggs.'"

"He says, 'No, you didn't.'"

"I say, 'Yeah, I did.'"

"He says, 'The guy you roughed up, genius, did he ever *say* he was Evan Briggs?'"

"So then I had to think back," Ralphie went on. "An' the truth is that I never really heard 'im admit it. So I say, 'But Tony, I was at his house, which Bert told me where it was.' And he says—due respect here—'Well, even Bert can make a mistake.'"

The old man petted his dog with one hand and nipped at his anisette with the other. Sounding sheepish, he said, "Jeez, I guess I did. Sorry. I didn't have an exact address. Just remembered the crypts an' the pool. Then again, the graveyard's fulla crypts, which goes wit' it bein' a graveyard after all, plus which, Flahda, there's lotsa houses wit' pools."

"Ah, don't worry about it," Ralphie said. "It's on me. I shoulda made sure. I was in too much of a hurry. Just wanted to get the goddamn beatin' over wit' and go see Darla and get a hug and some pancakes...So anyways, Tony's still cursin' me out and pacin' all around me, and he says, 'So, genius, do ya know who ya *did* beat up?' Well, what could I say to that? I mean, obviously I didn't know. So I just stand there lookin' like an idiot. He says, 'Well, I'll tell ya who ya beat up. Ya beat up my ghostwriter. A guy I'm countin' on. A guy I need. That's who you beat up, numbnuts.'"

"So he says this," Ralphie went on, "an' I'm standin' there feelin' like shit, and all I can manage to say is, 'Jeez, Tony, I guess I fucked up. I'm sorry.' An' he, like, mimics me. 'You're sorry. Well, fine. You're sorry. But you don't just need to say that to me. Ya need to say it to him.'

"'Him?' I say. 'Yeah,' he says. 'Richie Delinco. My ghostwriter. The guy ya beat up. You're gonna go back to his place and tell him how sorry y'are and you're gonna mop the floor wit' your tongue and ask him to forgive ya.' An' I say, 'Boss, please don't make me do that. It's like the most embarrassin' thing ever. I'll get all tongue-tied. I won't know what to say.' An' he says, 'Well, think a somethin', genius. I tol' him ya'd be there at six onna dot. Don't fuck up again.'"

Ralphie finished up his story, drained his anisette, and ground his teeth together. They made a sound like tires on a gravel driveway.

Bert refilled his guest's glass and said, "Jeez, havin' t'apologize to a guy ya just roughed up. That's harsh. Kinda humiliatin'."

"Just been a bastard of a day."

"Real bastard," Bert agreed. "Tell ya what, though. If it makes it any easier, the apology I mean, I'll go wit' ya if ya like. Richie's okay. I known him for years. Maybe I can sorta ease the way, help ya find some words or somethin'."

Ralphie brightened just a little and looked up from under knitted eyebrows. "Ya'd do that for me, Bert? That'd really be a solid."

"Sure, no problem," the old man said, cradling his dog as he eased up from his chair.

He went to the living room window, pulled back the curtain, and took a contemplative look across the roadway to the bustling promenade and the green ocean beyond. Then he said, "But ya know, the whole time you was talkin', I'm thinkin' about the who, why, and wherefore of all this trouble. The ghostwriter gets beat up. You get slapped. Tony's bowels are in an uproar. Why? I mean, if ya look past this or that detail and try to get to, say, the root cause or— what the hell's that Bible word? Genesis. The genesis of all this aggravation, meanin' where it starts from and who did what to who to get the whole frickin' ball a wax rollin' down the hillside, 'cept I guess it's snow, not wax, that rolls, 'cause wax is pretty sticky. But anyway, everything's gotta start somewhere, even like what they say about a hurricane wit' a butterfly and a grain a sand, which I never understood how that worked, so leave it onna side. But wit' our present situation, why is all this shit goin' on? Seems to me it all starts wit' some deadbeat named Harry Forest who don't pay his debts, then disappears, then tries ta work everyone around to doin' exactly what he wants to fix the mess that he fucked up inna first place. So everybody else is havin' a shitty day while this Harry guy is prob'ly soakin' inna hot tub and not doin' much a anything 'cept directin' traffic through the stinkin' chaos he has himself created. 'Zat seem fair to you?"

Ralphie tilted his head and let the words roll around in there a moment. Then he said, "Now that ya put it that way, fuck no."

"Fuck no is right. I mean, people say what goes 'round comes 'round, 'cept so far this ain't coming 'round to Harry, which is where it seems to me it has to come 'round to if it's gonna be logical and fair, otherwise it's gonna feel like one a those songs that don't end on the note it starts wit', so it don't sound finished and it leaves ya kinda antsy. See what I'm sayin'?"

"Didn't quite follow that last part," admitted Ralphie.

"Aw, doesn't matter. Just thinkin' out loud. Want another anisette while I'm gettin' ready? Takes me a while, y'unnerstand. Then we'll suck it up and get this damn apology over wit'."

TWENTY-EIGHT

It was a bit before six when Richie suddenly felt like going for a bike ride. It was the nicest time of day for it. The sun had lost its sting, the afternoon haze put a wisp of softening blur on the edges of fronds and houses, and the humidity lifted smells of jasmine and hot stones and ripening papayas in people's yards. At the beach, there would be a drowsy sense of daytime slouching gratefully toward evening, towels being shaken free of sand, tanned toes inching their way into flip-flops. So he rolled his old blue bike past the nudists in the compound and headed out. He didn't have a destination in mind. Or at least he didn't know he did. Or at least he didn't admit it.

Just around the same time, Darla felt an urge to have a stroll, a break from the cushy but stifling comforts of a nice hotel. She didn't think she had a destination either.

Yet they both ended up on the promenade by the Sno-Cone truck.

Darla arrived first and sat down on the seawall, watching the joggers and the skaters and the scooters going by. Richie trundled up barely half a minute after. He stopped the bike and straddled it. They looked at each other. She smiled and said, "You didn't run me over this time."

"You didn't jump out without looking."

She peered out at the sea a moment. "Did you know I'd be here?"

"Did you know I'd come riding along?"

"I asked you first," she said.

He pressed his lips together. "Guess I sort of knew. Or maybe was just hoping. Hard to tell the difference sometimes." He briefly glanced away from her and at the Sno-Cone truck. "Want one?"

"Yeah. But it's my turn. Pick your flavor."

He asked for lemon-lime.

"That's what you had last time," she said.

"What can I say? I know what I like."

"Must make life easier. I'm trying something different."

She stood up and went over to the truck. He climbed off his bike, rolled it to seawall, and sat down. She brought him his Sno-Cone. He asked what she'd decided on. She said raspberry. After she'd had some, he asked if it was any good. She said it didn't taste like raspberries, but it was pretty nice. And that just about used up the small talk.

After a couple more licks, she said, "Richie...What happened last night...Can we talk about it?"

"Well, yeah. Sure. If you like," he said, feeling a vague dread that there'd be remorse, regrets, recriminations, that something wonderful would end up coming around to a question of whose fault it was.

"You did me a big favor."

"I did? The pleasure was all mine."

"No. Actually a lot of it was mine. Even-steven. Which surprised the heck out of me, if you want the truth. And the other surprise, not a total surprise, is that it finally made me realize I'm not in love with Ralphie, because what happened wouldn't have happened if I was, because that's not the way I am. I don't kiss guys and get carried away if I'm in love with someone else. I guess I had to test myself to figure that out."

"Happy to be part of the experiment."

"I don't mean it that way. You know I don't. I'm just trying to think it through and work out where that leaves us."

"Well, for the moment," he said, gesturing broadly out across the ocean, "it leaves us sitting here on the seawall, eating Sno-Cones."

"For the moment. And it's kind of terrific. But let's be practical."

"Do we have to? I kind of hate the concept."

"Me too. But still...Richie, are you in love with me? I mean, really in love?"

He had just squeezed a clot of ice toward the top of his paper cup and was about to take a nibble of it. Instead, he drew his lips away and let the ice subside again. But he couldn't come up with a ready answer fast enough, still less an answer he was sure about, so Darla went on.

"No, you're not. At least I hope you're not. And I don't think I'm really in love with you either. Or maybe it's just that I don't want to be. Or maybe we could get to be if we had the time. In love I mean. But I don't think we do have the time. I mean, you have your life down here and I have my life up there, and we're really incredibly different from each other, so how about if we just agree that it's been one of life's great flings, and we both feel good about it, and we can remember it as one of those secrets that always make you smile? Would that be okay?"

Richie didn't have a ready or a certain answer to that one either.

"Come on," she urged. "Tell me it's okay with you, 'cause it was really hard for me to say."

He looked down at the seawall, felt a pang swell up then gradually settle like a wake from a boat that was heading somewhere else and never coming back, and he finally managed to mumble something about how it was probably the smartest way to look at it and the best idea and if she felt all right about it then it was fine with him.

"Good," she said. "You sure?"

"No. Not really. I don't know if I'm sure or not. Takes me a while to sort things out. Sometimes I'm a little slow."

"Part of your charm," she said, letting out a deep breath and doing her best to smile before having a bite of Sno-Cone. "But for right now, how about we just decide we're pals, and if that's okay, then maybe as a friend you can help me figure something out."

"Sure, if I can."

She looked out at the flat green water. "So what the hell should I do about Ralphie?"

TWENTY-NINE

At that moment, already cringing, Ralphie was climbing the two steps up to the narrow porch of the house on Angela Street. When he reached the front door, he paused and looked back across his shoulder at Bert, who had gathered up Nacho and was holding the small creature against his belly like a football. Bert gave the big man an encouraging nod, and he knocked.

Evan's voice called out. "Come on in. It's open."

Bert said nothing, though he found it slightly strange that a man who'd been ambushed in his own foyer that very morning would be so welcoming in tone and so cavalier about an unlocked door.

Ralphie turned the knob and pushed.

The door moved easily until it was about two-thirds open, then it hit resistance, at which point Evan sprang out from behind it. In his right hand, at chin level, he held a twelve-inch butcher knife. In his left he held a jumbo can of Raid, his index finger on the spray button.

Ralphie stopped in his tracks. Bert drifted another step forward and walked into the big man's back, the dog lightly sandwiched between them. "What the fuck?" said Ralphie.

"You're not going to get the drop on me twice," said Evan. "Not in the same day, for Christ's sake."

By then, Bert had slid off to the side and could peek around the bulk of Ralphie's torso. He saw the raised knife. He saw the lifted can. He said, "Yeah, but cockroach stuff?"

"Best I had on hand," said Evan. He waggled the knife and rattled the can, or maybe he was trembling.

The absurd standoff went on for several seconds, until Bert said, "Okay, okay, calm down. You made your point. Round two goes to you by unanimous decision. But can we please cut out the pest control routine? Ralphie heah has just come t'apologize."

The big man raised his arms in a gesture of surrender.

Evan glanced at him then turned back to Bert. "So why the hell are *you* here?"

Nacho didn't like the tone of that. He started up a noise that wasn't quite a snarl, more like a rasping gurgle from the back of his narrow throat.

"Ambassador a goodwill," Bert said.

"Goodwill my eye," said Evan.

Ralphie watched the other two men glaring at each other and said, "Hey, youse guys on the outs or somethin'? Bert kinda said you was old friends."

With a sideways look at Evan, Bert said, "We are. Aren't we...Richie? Been in a little bit of a rough patch lately. We'll get past it, won't we?"

Evan said nothing but he lowered his arms and stepped aside to let his guests move deeper into the house. Ralphie didn't quite show his back as he sidled by. Evan stepped into the kitchen, put the knife in a drawer and the insect bomb beneath the sink, then, fastidious as ever, took a moment to wash the bad smell off his hands.

In the living room, he found his guests still standing up. Ralphie softly and humbly asked if they could sit, and Evan finally realized that he was now safe and in control. He was under Tony's protection. He was untouchable. He began to relish the situation. He said, "My, aren't we polite this evening? Such a nice contrast with earlier today."

He half-smiled and gestured toward the furniture. Everyone sat. Ralphie stayed on the very edge of his chair. There was a silence. Bert cleared his throat. There was more silence. Ralphie's face started twisting up like he was trying to form words, but nothing came out. Finally, Bert said, "Ralphie's very sorry for the unfortunate incident this morning that resulted in your gettin' knocked around a little bit."

"Thank you," said Evan. "Very nice. But the apology would strike me as a great deal more sincere if it came from the individual who did the knockin' around, as you so quaintly put it."

He stared at Ralphie. The big man squirmed and flushed. His hands fidgeted and his lips contorted. His neck swelled in his collar. Evan watched him suffer and reflected on the amazing range of ways that revenge could be exacted. Finally the big man managed to say, "Look, I'm very sorry. I messed up bad. Shouldn't't'a happened. I apologize."

Evan shrugged with just a slight tease of acceptance. "Well, stuff happens. To err is human..."

Bert said, "Please don't start wit' the Shakespeare shit."

"It isn't Shakespeare, it's Pope. Alexander."

"I don't care which pope it is. Don't say nothin' bad 'bout the Cat'lic church."

Evan frowned, then, milking the sweet moment of being sucked up to, he started over. "To err is human, to forgive divine. But I might find it easier to forgive if I knew just how and why this little *faux pas* happened."

Ralphie looked at Bert. Bert scratched the dog and looked at Ralphie. Finally the big man said, "Well, I thought you was the other guy."

With pretended naiveté, Evan said, "Other guy?"

"Evan Briggs. The one that writes the dead guy's books and's been foolin' around wit' Darla."

"Oh, *that* guy," said Evan. He cast an acid glance at Bert while continuing to talk to Ralphie. "What made you think he lives here?"

Bert said, "Um, that wasn't Ralphie's fault. That's my fault. Ya want my apology, too? Okay, Richie, ya got it. Chalk it up. I had the wrong parta Angela Street. Like the pope says, to err is human."

Evan took that in with his anchovy-lipped smile and a narrowing of his eyes. He crossed and recrossed his legs while teetering for some seconds on the brink of a betrayal. He himself had taken a beating that morning. Why? Because Bert and the real Richie, for their own convenience, had set him up. They'd conspired to steer this enforcer to his house. Why shouldn't he return the favor? Why the hell should he shield the guy who hadn't shielded him? Why should he be the only one taking punishment? He wrestled with his conscience for a moment. His conscience lost.

"Geez, Bert," he said at last, "for a person who knows Key West so well, you were way off on the address. I happen to know where Evan Briggs lives, and it's nowhere close to Angela Street."

The words took a heartbeat to sink in then seemed to galvanize Ralphie. His expression changed from hangdog to avid. His posture reinflated. "So where's he live?"

"Eight, ten blocks from here. Little street called Watson." Then, with a smirk, he added, "In a nudist colony."

"Nudist colony? And he's messin' wit' Darla?"

Evan shrugged.

The big man said, "You know where that street is, Bert?"

Stalling, Bert petted the dog and said, "Um, sorta. Gen'rally. Don't know nothin' about a nudist camp."

"Shouldn't be too hard to find," goaded Evan.

Ralphie started lifting from his seat. "Shit, come on, let's go right now. Lemme get the job the hell over wit'. Do it right this time."

Evan said, "By all means, do it right. But sit down, please. We haven't quite finished our business here."

Ralphie was twitchy but he sat. "What else?"

"I haven't yet accepted your apology."

"But I've said it. I goofed. I fucked up. I erred or however ya say it. I'm very, very sorry."

"Thank you. Now I accept. Give my regards to Evan Briggs."

THIRTY

Ralphie barreled down the porch steps and onto the skinny pavement of Angela Street. With the cemetery fence and the blockish crypts looming close in front of him, he turned to Bert and said, "Okay, so where's this Watson Street?"

The old man gestured vaguely toward the far side of the graveyard. "Kinda the other side a town."

"So let's cut through," the eager big man said.

"Locked at night."

Ralphie grabbed and shook a couple of the iron posts but quickly realized they were not the kind he could bend. "So let's go 'round. Left or right?"

Bert cupped his chin in his hand and very deliberately peered first in one direction then the other. At some point in his swiveling around, he noticed a simple mailbox on a post. On the flap of the mailbox, in extremely tidy lettering, was a name. BRIGGS. The old man flicked Nacho's leash. The dog lurched like a tiny buggy horse being urged along. Bert pretended to be tugged over half a step to hide the mailbox. Then he said, "Either way it's a long walk, Ralphie. You sure ya wanna do this now?"

"Shit, yeah. Got the fuckin' apology over wit', got a heada steam built up, I wanna get it done."

In his most avuncular tone, Bert said, "I'm just a little worried that it might not be the best idea to be in so much of a hurry. 'Member what happened last time ya was in too much of a hurry?"

He paused. By reflex, Ralphie reached up and touched his cheek. The feel of Tony's rings was long gone. The humiliation wasn't.

"That's right," Bert resumed. "Ya got slapped. And I'd hate to see ya get slapped again."

"But this time I know I'm right."

"Ya thought that last time, too. Besides, we don't have the exact address on Watson Street. Whadda we do, knock on doors and see if someone answers naked? And on toppa that, are ya even sure Tony's still onboard wit' this?"

"Well, sure, he said—"

"Said when?" Bert interrupted. "Yesterday? This afternoon? Things change fast sometimes. I was you, I'd slow down a little and at least make sure—"

Ralphie's phone started ringing. The old man was running low on stalling tactics and was glad for the distraction.

The big man fished his phone out of a pocket. He looked at the incoming number and his fighting face quickly recomposed itself into a gentle, even moony expression. "Hello, baby," he purred. "Everything okay?"

It didn't take long for his features to rearrange themselves again when he heard the answer. His eyes drooped a little at the outside corners. His lips puffed out toward a pout. He said, "Well, okay, baby, sure...Now?...Well, fine, if it's important...Yeah, anyplace. Just name it...Okay, I'll find it. See ya soon."

He clicked out of the call and put the phone away. He didn't need to tell Bert who the caller was. He just said, "She says we gotta talk."

"Talkin's good."

"Sometimes. Sometimes not. I ain't the world's best at it."

"So, youse are gonna meet?"

"Yeah. Place called the Eclipse Saloon. Know it?"

"Know it? I practically live there. It's right down on Simonton. Tell 'em I sent ya. They'll treat ya good."

"Thanks," said the big man. Then, after being in such a hurry to get on with his business, he just lingered a long moment, shifting weight from foot to foot at the edge of a cone of streetlight next to the cemetery fence. "I don't think this is gonna be a happy talk, Bert."

"Hey, ya never know. Maybe it'll clear the air, whatever. Main thing is, give 'er your full attention. This other shit, forget it for a while. This other shit can wait, *capeesh*?"

Ralphie nodded but by then he was only half-listening, thinking ahead to seeing Darla, the thing he most wanted and most dreaded. Absently, he said, "I dunno, Bert. Maybe it'll turn out fine. But the way she sounded, I got this sick feelin' way down in my gut. I think she's gonna dump me."

Not even Bert knew what to say to that. He just gave Ralphie a comradely pat on the shoulder and the two men walked off in opposite directions.

🦀 🦀 🦀

At Antonia's, on Duval Street, prosperous diners were leaning over linen tablecloths and twinkling glassware as they twirled fettuccine or coaxed stone crabs from their shells. At a small table near the back, Harry Forest was expertly using the tip of his knife to hollow out the round bone in the center of his *osso buco,* making sure to scrape out every last morsel of the succulent, translucent marrow. His mouth not quite empty, his eyes half-closed in enjoyment, he said, "Try getting this in Helsinki. Reindeer maybe. Veal, no way."

Tony Totes, midway through a relatively abstemious dinner of linguine and clams, regarded his tablemate's lip-smacking gusto with a mix of envy and slight disgust. "You always were a bit of a glutton."

"I prefer gourmand," said Harry, turning his attention to a mound of creamy polenta. "It's life, Tony. If you like something, why not have a lot of it? Feel like another bottle of this amusing Amarone?"

"Who's buying?"

"I am," said the author.

"Yeah, wit' house money."

Harry laughed, lifted the empty bottle, gestured to the waiter, then turned back to Tony. "Tell you what. I'll keep picking up the tabs even when we're all squared up."

Tony said nothing. He had grave and mocking doubts as to whether that would ever happen. In fact, he couldn't quite remember the last time he truly believed that Harry would ever make good on his debt. Even now, even if everything went Harry's way, even if he got his job back—chances are he'd find a new set of excuses to stall, to dodge...It's not like he, Tony, didn't know that. So where was the line between wanting to believe and just plain kidding yourself like every other sucker?

Breaking in on the other man's thoughts, Harry said, "And speaking of squaring up, how's our problem-solving going?"

Tony twirled some linguine then put the forkful down again. "Not great. There's been a complication."

"Complication? I thought it all seemed pretty simple."

Tony leaned in a little closer. "Well, it isn't. Ralphie beat up the wrong guy."

Harry laughed. He had a wad of polenta in his gullet and he had to press his napkin hard against his lips to keep it from coming up again.

Tony said, "Ain't funny when a guy gets beat up, Harry. Y'ever been beat up?"

The other man shrugged. "Junior high school, maybe."

"Don't count. Y'ever been beat up as a grown-up? As a man?"

"No. My business, people don't throw punches. They write reviews. Pretty much comes down to the same thing."

"Bullshit," said Tony. "If you'd ever been beat up, you'd know the difference sure as hell. And maybe you'd have a little more sympathy for what the next poor schnook is feeling, and maybe you'd have a better sense of when you should or shouldn't laugh."

Harry put his napkin back in his lap. Half kidding but half not, he said, "You scolding me, Tony?"

Tony said nothing and went back to his pasta. The waiter brought over the fresh bottle of wine and showed the label and did the whole routine. Harry swirled it, tasted, and approved. The waiter poured.

Hoping to lighten the mood, the author raised his glass and said, "Here's to better days, both past and future."

Tony joined in the toast but he wasn't quite so sure about the future part. Behind a grudging and melancholy smile, he was trying to remember just exactly why he used to like this guy so goddamn much.

THIRTY-ONE

Bert was winded by the time he reached the compound on Watson Street. He knocked on the gate and was about to holler out Richie's name when it suddenly swung open. Behind it stood a naked man in Crocs. Judging by his scaly knees and the exhausted stretch of his scrotum, he seemed not too much younger than Bert himself. He smiled at the visitor and his dog and said, "Namaste."

Bert said, "And back at ya."

"Hot yoga?"

"'Scuse me?"

"You're here for class?"

"Um, no."

"It's pay-what-you-wish."

"Thanks. It's not about the money."

"Well-behaved dogs are welcome."

"Thanks. It's not about the dog."

"I think you'd find it very invigorating."

"Listen, no offense, Mahatma, but if I get any more invigorated, I'll plotz. I'm just here to see a friend."

"Ah. Welcome." The other man put his palms together, slightly bowed his head, and stepped aside. He had a nice smell of menthol and eucalyptus about him, but it made Nacho sneeze as they slid past.

Through the screen door of the yellow cottage, Bert could see Richie sitting at his desk and tapping on his keyboard. "Yo," he called out. "Still working?"

Turning around with the slightly glazed expression of someone who's been looking at a screen too long, Richie said, "Oh hi, Bert." Rising from his chair and heading to the door, he went on. "Yeah, still working. Nice thing about a made-up story. Takes your mind off the other shit."

Before he'd even stepped over the threshold, Bert said, "Well, sorry, but your mind's about to get snapped back to the other shit, because your buddy Evan just ratted you out."

"What?"

"I'll explain, but do I have to stand here inna doorway like fuckin' FedEx? I'd like to siddown an' I'd appreciate some water for the dog."

Richie gestured his friend toward the floral sofa that had seen more traffic in the last two days than in a typical six months, then he went to the kitchen and filled a bowl with water. He put the bowl on the floor next to Nacho. Nacho wouldn't drink from it. Bert said, "Ya got somethin' metal? More like a regular dog bowl?"

"I don't have a dog. Why would I have a dog bowl?"

"Outa basic consideration for guests. But the hell with it. Dog gets thirsty enough, he'll condescend. And by the way, the reason he's thirsty is that we practically sprinted over here from Angela Street ta give ya a heads-up that Evan just told Ralphie where ya live."

The news, at first, didn't rattle Richie very much. "Only fair," he said, "we did the same to him."

"True," said Bert, "but the two situations ain't exactly parallel or, what's that word, anagalous—"

"Analogous?"

"Correct. Meanin' when there's two things that are sorta alike but not totally alike, 'cause no two things are ever totally alike, which leaves lotsa room for heated and often pointless arguments about how alike they are or aren't, and which is more important, the sameness or the difference. And in many cases, let's face it, who gives a rat's ass anyways, 'cause it's just two guys tryin' to sound smarter than the other guy and comin' up wit' angles and minutiae, however ya say it, that the other guy didn't think of. Fuck 'em, let 'em argue. However, inna current instance, it happens to be clear as the palm a your hand that the difference is way more important, 'cause when Ralphie roughed up Evan, he was just doin' his job. But by now he's very pissed off and it's very personal. He's been slapped across the kisser by his boss. He's had to apologize to a guy he don't respect and who played it like an asshole and really rubbed it in. And he thinks his girlfriend is about to give 'im the old heave-ho."

"Well, I think he's right about that," said Richie.

"Ah, so you are, let's say, privy to the young lady's inmost thoughts?"

"We've talked."

Bert bent down and scooped up Nacho, who apparently was not thirsty enough to drink from a bowl he didn't like. "You've talked. Very discreet. Very chivalrous. But it's starting to sound more than a little bit like you've alienated her affections, aka stolen her from right out under his nose."

"Not true, Bert. It's not about me. She just figured out she doesn't love him enough."

"And this just happened to occur when she was hangin' out wit' you. Coincidence?"

"Not saying that, exactly—"

"But look," Bert interrupted, "whatever the exact truth of it is, wit' all its emotional subtleties and romantic nuance as always pertains when somebody falls in or outa love or between the sheets at least, how's it gonna look to him? One day he has a girlfriend. She goes to Key West, spends a little time wit' a local guy, then boom, he ain't got the girlfriend no more. Plus he's been slapped and made to grovel, and on toppa that, the guy who did or didn't steal the girlfriend is also perceived, albeit they got it ass backwards, to be a business problem for his boss, and he's embarrassed that so far he's done a shitty job a fixin' the problem. So ya put it all together, and the obvious conclusion is that he's extremely pissed off and you're in big trouble, my friend."

Richie sat and took that in. Bert bent down, scooped up a handful of water, and gave it to the dog. After a moment he went on.

"So, you gonna end up wit' 'er?"

"Hm?"

"The girlfriend. Darla. If ya happen ta survive this mess, think you'll be an item?"

The younger man pursed his lips and gave a small, slow shake to his head. "Nah. That isn't what she wants. She's smart. She's practical. She thinks it wouldn't work out."

"Okay, fine. And whadda you think?"

Richie panned absently around the living room and nibbled briefly on his knuckles. "I don't really know. She did most of the talking. What she said made sense. I just sort of went along."

Bert nodded and scratched the dog's head. "Ya know," he said, "it's been a helluva long time since I was what you might call involved wit' women, but as far as I can tell, some things just don't change. Did it ever occur to you, while she was bein' practical and smart and you weren't doin' or sayin' much a anything, that maybe she was feelin' you out to see how much you cared? Or maybe lettin' you off the hook? Givin' you an out that maybe she hoped you wouldn't take?"

"I don't know, Bert. She's pretty direct."

"An' you lean a little wishy-washy sometimes, no offense. Just sayin' maybe the message wasn't quite as simple as it sounded. But anyways, be that as it may, we got more pressin' things to deal wit', mainly that Ralphie might be on his way here even as I keep yakkin', and it would be a great deal better for your health if you was not around."

Richie blinked at the confines of his bungalow and silently agreed that it would be a bad place to be cornered. "So where am I supposed to go?"

"That's a problem," Bert said. "Not a lotta places to hide in our little town. Not for long, at least. Besides, hidin' out would only be a short-term strategy. Wouldn't really fix nothin'. Not wit' all the cockamamie misunderstandin's we got flyin' back and fort'. They ain't gonna get cleared up by hidin' out, or by this guy beats up that guy, or a coupla guys have a private sitdown wit' cigars, or Tony gives out orders wit'out he really knows what's goin' on. The only way it gets settled is if we find a way to bring everyone together—"

"Which would totally wreck the book-swap plan," Richie blurted.

"Maybe, maybe not. But first things first. I mean, book deal don't help ya if you're dead. Plus which, we got the problem that not everyone's gonna be thrilled to take a meetin' wit' everybody else, considerin' the bad feelin' and mistrust that have already arisen or arose or erupted or however ya say it. So it'll take a certain amount a tactics and subterfuge and persuadin' to bring everyone along, so I guess I gotta get my gun."

"Your gun? Bert, you wouldn't—"

"What? Shoot someone? Hope not. But the nice thing about the gun is that it sorta helps ya be the emcee. Kinda keep a lid onna proceedings."

"What proceedings? Bert, this is moving awfully fast for me."

"Like it isn't for me?" the old man said. "I'm givin' myself palpitootions heah. But it's sorta comin' to me piece by piece. Like now I suddenly think I got the place."

"The place for what?"

"Ain't you been listenin'? For the get-together. The whaddyacallit, confrontation. It's this weird spot a few miles up the Keys. I brought Ralphie up there a coupla days ago when I was massagin' 'im for information. Half-built bridge. Abandoned. Deserted. Years ago, I saw two yeggs sink a Buick there."

"A Buick?"

"Yeah, a Buick. Sedan. Point is, there's nobody around. Bridge sticks outa the undergrowth like a plank. Fast water underneath. If someone's gotta go...well, ya get the picture."

Richie swallowed hard but couldn't speak.

Bert licked his flubbery lips. "Ah, an' one other thing just came to me. Plan like this, ya can't just go waggin' a gun in people's faces. Ya gotta give 'em an incentive to go along. An inducement. Some whaddyacallit...Bait."

"Bait?"

"Yeah. Ya know. Bait. Somethin' that kinda dangles out there."

"I know what bait means, Bert. So what's it gonna be?"

The old man scratched the dog. "It ain't gonna be a *what,* Richie. It's gonna be a who. Ain't it obvious? You."

Richie lightly tapped his breastbone and said, "Me?"

"Who else? Who's the guy Ralphie's so hot to meet? Who's the guy writin' Harry's book right now? Who's the guy that's s'posed to be doin' Tony's memoir? Who's the guy that Darla can't make up her mind about? You, you, you, and you."

"But—"

"But what?" said Bert, as he started wriggling and pushing himself up from the squishy cushion of the floral sofa. "Look, it's our best shot at gettin' this craziness cleared up. I'll give ya directions to the place. Grab a cab. Settle in. Sit tight. Relax."

"Relax. Right."

The old man gathered up the dog and headed to the bungalow doorway. "Oh, and one more thing," he said when he was halfway through it. "Bug juice. Load up good before ya go. Head ta toe. Everywhere."

THIRTY-TWO

Ralphie got to the Eclipse first and took a small, dim table to the left of the bar, under a mounted sailfish from back in the days when anglers kept their catch, had it stuffed, and hung it on a wall in the rec room with a brass plaque saying how big it was. A server came over. Ralphie told her he was a friend of Bert's, he was having one of the worst days of his entire life, and could he please have a double J&B. She brought him a drink you could have drowned a palm rat in.

He was a third of the way through it when Darla showed up. She wore a dark blouse buttoned almost to the throat and shorts that came down almost to her knees. If she was trying not to look especially appealing, it didn't work on Ralphie. He still thought she was gorgeous. He stifled the urge to stand up and hug her because he didn't want to get shot down again. He just pulled a chair back for her and she sat. The server came over and she ordered white wine. When it arrived, they clinked glasses, but Ralphie was clutching his too hard for it to ring.

She took a sip, then put the wine down and fiddled with the edge of her cardboard coaster. Finally she said, "Ralphie, we've had some real nice times together. I like you a lot."

"Already I don't like the sound of that."

"And I don't want to hurt your feelings."

"Y'already have. By now I'm gettin' used to it, at least."

"I'm sorry."

If being apologized to was supposed to feel any less lousy than having to apologize, it didn't. He drank some Scotch and kept quiet for a moment. Then he said, "So we're through?"

She licked her lips, lowered her eyes, and nodded.

"This new guy. Ya like 'im that much?"

"That's not what it's about."

"No? Then what the hell is it about?"

"It's complicated, Ralphie. I'm still trying to sort it all out. My time here. Such a different place. Made me see things different. Being so tied in with all my Daddy stuff. Tied to New York, old habits. Tied to the same old version of being me..."

The complications didn't seem to hold Ralphie's attention for very long. He tried to listen but his mind kept spiraling down to one simple thing that was gradually nudging him from hurt to angry. He said, "Ya slept with 'im?"

"That's nobody's business."

"I'll take that as a yes."

She reached out to touch his hand. He yanked his arm away.

"Ralphie," she said, "I don't want this to be ugly. That part of it so doesn't matter."

"Does to me. You cheated on me, Darla."

"No I didn't. Cheating is when you're in a relationship and you fool around. I was already out of our relationship. My mind was made up. I knew I wasn't going back to you."

"So you could fuck this writer wit' a clear conscience. Very convenient."

"Do we have to be crude? Does it make you feel any better?"

He ignored that. Wounded pride had soured by then into full-on rage, and he was being swept along in the surge like a broken stick. "Prob'ly pretty convenient for him, too. One more tourist girl wit' loose panties. Get laid a time or two, she flies away, he's ready for the next batch—"

"That isn't how it was—"

"'Cept maybe there ain't gonna be a next batch for this guy. Maybe this guy's not gonna be in any kinda shape to mess wit' tourist girls. Or do mucha anything else either."

"Don't be hateful, Ralphie. Please?"

He smirked at that. "Hateful? Me? Nah. I take this guy out, I'd just be doin' my job. Yeah. You think you're the only one who can play a little trick on your conscience and then do exactly what you feel like? I can do that too. I can pretend this has nothin' to do wit' you. Nothin' personal. Jus' doin' what I get paid for. By your father. And enjoyin' every second for a change."

"Come on, Ralphie. You wouldn't enjoy hurting him. You'd hate yourself. You're better than that."

"Yeah, guess I'm a fuckin' prince. So why'd ya dump me then?"

"Look, there is no why. I just don't want people to be hurt, okay?" She looked down, fretted with her coaster, rolled shreds of it beneath her fingertips. "Remember when I asked you—"

"Yeah, I remember exactly. You asked me if there was ever a time when your father tol' me to do somethin' and you begged me not to, would I do it anyway. Very tough question. Really tough. But here's the thing, Darla. You had leverage then. A lot. Now you don't. Ya know what happened to your leverage? You fucked it away. I hope it was worth it for you."

He gave her a sideways look full of spite and sorrow, drained his drink, slammed the glass down, reached into a pocket, dropped a fifty on the table, and walked out. Darla sat there for a couple minutes under the stuffed and mounted fish. She knew that nothing good could come of chasing him.

.

THIRTY-THREE

B ack at the Paradiso, Bert's first order of business was to fill the scratched and dented stovetop pot in which he made his espresso. The evening ahead would call for maximum alertness, so he packed the fine-ground coffee extra tight. Then he lit the stove and went to the bedroom closet where he kept his antique .38.

He found it at the back of the drawer with the driving gloves and balled up socks. He also found the ankle holster with the fraying leather straps and tarnished buckles. He brought the things into the breakfast nook and laid them on the boomerang pattern dinette table under a lamp with a Sputnik design. Resting his foot on a chair, he raised his pants leg and began securing the holster around his bony calf. This used to be something he could do with his eyes closed, just a quick series of automatic gestures. But now his knee required some finessing to make it flex to a convenient angle and his blunt fingers needed several tries at threading the straps through the buckles. By the time the gun was snugly stashed and his trousers readjusted, the coffee was boiling over.

He wiped the gritty brown foam from the stovetop and poured out the espresso.

In the living room, he settled into his favorite chair while Nacho dragged mangled squeak toys—a headless chicken, a frog with no legs—from underneath the furniture. He switched on the TV and pretended to watch a cop show while waiting for Ralphie.

Two commercials later, there was a knock on the door. It wasn't exactly a hammering but it was louder than polite. Bert answered it. A disheveled Ralphie stood there in the frame. He smelled of Scotch and anger, with just a stale hint of the cologne he claimed to use only sparingly. Ushering him in, Bert said, "How'd it go?"

"Shitty."

"Want some coffee?"

"Sure, why not."

The big man perched on the edge of a sofa. When Bert brought in his lukewarm demi-tasse, he said, "Thanks. She dumped me. Like I thought she would."

Easing down into his seat, Bert said, "Ah, I'm sorry. I mean, I guess I'm sorry. Who knows? Maybe it's for the best."

"Sure don't feel that way."

"I get it. Then again, there's always a bright side. My age, ya look for the bright side or why the fuck else would ya get outa bed? I mean, nothin' against Darla, but bein' wit' the boss's daughter makes things complicated. What if ya wanna quit? What if someone makes ya a better offer? What if ya wanna change careers?"

"To what? Fuck else am I gonna do, Bert? Website design?"

"Fair point. But at least you're freed up now. Like I say, I'm looking for a bright spot." He finished his coffee and put the cup aside. "And what about the other thing? Watson Street. Ya find the place?"

"Another disaster," said Ralphie, curling his lips and shaking his head. "So I find the street, no problem. I'm walkin' up and down, tryin' to figure which is the nudie place, peekin' in windows like a fuckin' pervert. Finally I see a gate and hear some voices. So I push it open. There's a swimmin' pool and a buncha naked people standin' on their heads."

"On their heads?"

"Yeah. Yoga or some shit. It was disgustin'. Men, women, everything just hangin' upside down. I mean everything. I mean hangin'. It was gross. So I say I'm lookin' for this writer guy and they point me to a little shithole of a place. Except the guy ain't home. I kinda quietly break the door down, look around, smash a couple things, and that's it. That's all the satisfaction I got. One more thing that went completely lousy these last coupla days."

"Tough stretch," said Bert, and nodded sympathetically. "Guess it all kinda started when ya beat up the wrong guy."

Ralphie just looked down at the floor.

"Except, if it makes ya feel any better, ya didn't."

"Huh?"

The old man reached a hand down and softly snapped his fingers. Nacho came running over and he lifted the small creature to his lap. "Listen, Ralphie, there's a few things need some clearin' up," he said. "Like, for starters, the guy you thought was Evan Briggs? Well, he is Evan Briggs."

Ralphie's face was blank except for a sheaf of vertical lines between his eyebrows. "You messin' wit' my head, Bert?"

"Nah. Straight skinny. The name's right there onna mailbox. Briggs. You had it right. Tony has it wrong."

"But—"

Bert fended off the interruption with a lifted hand. "It'll get explained in due time, but inna meanwhile I'll tell ya somethin' else. The guy you're so mad at, who Tony thinks is Evan Briggs? Well, he's really Richie Delinco, and he happens to be a friend of mine. Plus which, I happen to know exactly where he is right now."

The big man swelled up at that. "You know? Jeez, Bert, I thought—"

"Thought what? That I was on your side? I am. But I'm on Richie's side, too. Mainly, what side I'm on is that I don't wanna see good people get hurt onna basis of misunderstandin's that coulda been rectified, i.e., solved, if people would just shut up and talk to each other. So I got a deal t'offer ya. I will take ya to where Richie is, but only if we round up all the innerested parties and go together so that everybody gets clued in and gets to have their say, and if everybody, especially you, promises not to be a hothead, and as long as it's understood that I'm packin'—"

"Y'are?"

Bert twitched up his pants leg just enough to show the .38.

"—And that I'm the only one that's packin', and that I will take all necessary steps if things get outa hand 'cause someone starts actin' like a hothead. Is this acceptable to you?"

THIRTY-FOUR

Tony Totes had taken some Maalox and was brooding on his balcony at Flagler House. His dinner wasn't settling all that well, and he suspected it was because he'd been annoyed and sad while he was eating it. It didn't used to be that way. His digestion used to be perfect when he dined with Harry. The laughs helped it along. The funny stories paced out the meal. The table-hopping visits from other high-class artsy types made everything go down easy. At least that's how he remembered it. Then again, as he was admitting to himself more and more each day, it had been a hell of a lot easier to be nostalgic about the good old days with Harry when Harry was still dead. This time around, his old friend's smug charm and unkind wit seemed to be wearing very thin, like a suit of clothes that had been tailored long ago and made to fit a younger man.

He was glad to be distracted from his baleful thoughts by the ringing of his phone. He ID'd the caller and said, "Yeah, Bert. What's up?"

"What's up is that I can't really tell ya what's up right this very second, but I'm hopin' you'll agree to take a little ride wit' me and Ralphie."

"A ride? Now? What the fuck?"

"Just a short one. Car'll be crowded, but we're not goin' very far, and I think it'll be worth the trouble. Hopin' we'll come away wit' answers to a few naggin' questions."

"Like what?"

"Like, for instance, why can't your stud ghostwriter do an interview worth shit and doesn't even know what the vig is? And why is Ralphie havin' such a tough time figurin' out who to beat on? And why did Darla break up wit' 'im?"

"They broke up?"

"Ya didn't know?"

"Nah. She's been locked in her room the whole time I been home. Has her moods. Ya know."

"Who doesn't?" said Bert. "Well, look, not that I think you or anybody else can tell Darla what to do or not do, but ya might wanna mention that maybe she'd like to get her two cents in and possibly have some influence over certain outcomes. I think she'll want in. We'll be over there in ten, twelve minutes."

☝ ☝ ☝

Bert streamlined the preparations and got ready in record time. He just coaxed the glen plaid snap-brim driving cap down between Nacho's oversize ears, then pulled on his own to match. He found the car keys on the very first try and remembered to put the condo keys in a different pocket. He was operating at peak efficiency. It might have been the coffee.

Ralphie, meanwhile, had done a quick wash-up and put on fresh cologne that made the dog sneeze. The sneeze shook its cap off-center. Bert repositioned it just so.

At the Flagler House, Tony and his daughter were waiting under the *porte cochere*. Tony got the front, of course, so Ralphie moved into the back with Darla. They sat at opposite ends of the wide bench seat and didn't speak. As the old Caddy rounded the driveway and headed crosstown on Reynolds Street, Tony said, "So you wanna tell me what this is all about?"

"Not really," said the old man, petting the dog with the hand that wasn't on the wheel.

"Well, I hope you know what the hell you're doin'."

"I hope so, too. 'Cause there might have to be some kidnappin' involved."

"Kidnapping?" said Darla.

"Well, I'm not sure everyone's gonna be as easygoin' and openminded about goin' for a ride as youse. I mean, let's face it, TV, inna movies, goin' for a ride has, like, negative conjugations, connotations, whatever. Like ya go for a ride and it's the last place y'ever go. Happens, let's face it. So some people might be, let's say, a little reluctant, a little squeamish. Might need some persuadin'. That's all I'm sayin'."

They were skirting the cemetery by then. The moonlight was bright enough to throw hard-edged shadows from the mausolea and to echo the defeated angles of headstones beaten down by decade after decade of wind and rain, their loving inscriptions gradually scoured into drips like tear-tracks and flecks like skin with poison ivy. Bert eased onto Angela Street and stopped the car in front of the mailbox labeled BRIGGS.

Tony read the name and said, "So this is where that prick Evan lives?"

"Yes and no," said Bert, as he slowly bent down and freed the .38 from its holster on his leg.

"Fuck's that supposed to mean? He lives here or he don't."

"Says you." The old man gave the chihuahua what seemed to be a good-luck rub and opened the driver's side door.

By reflex and long experience, Ralphie made a move to climb out of the car and come along to help, but Bert gestured him back into his seat. "This one I'll handle myself," he said. "Shouldn't be too taxin'. But don't worry, Ralphie, you'll get your opportunity. I promise."

The bugs were after Richie from the moment he stepped out of the Uber at the end of the road that led to the abandoned bridge. A blind man could have named the different insects from their sounds alone. The veering buzz of blue bottle flies. The rising whine of mosquitoes as they dive-bombed toward your ears. The drone of dragonflies, the click and clatter of grasshoppers, the violin-bow scratch of crickets, and above all the insane crescendo of cicadas amping up then drooping like a one-chord symphony written by a madman. Where the scarred pavement petered out and the undergrowth took over, there was added the lamb-like bleating of tree toads and the damp slither of geckos and chameleons sliding through the carpet of half-rotted leaves. Now and then there was the scrape of claws biting into tree bark as iguanas climbed in search of eggs.

Richie stepped carefully through the snaggling vines and the sedges that could slice through skin. Stunted casuarinas and peeling gumbo-limbos drank up most of the moonlight; where bright shafts filtered through, they were filled with dust and wings. Up ahead there were the remains of a barricade, now nothing more than a web of bleached-out boards, and beyond it stretched the futile bridge, dangling over empty air and rushing water, its long-ago ambition squelched, yearning for the other side that it would never reach.

He stepped around the barrier. The thwarted roadway felt diseased and spongy underfoot. He tested it board by board as he advanced. Lengths of splintery railing randomly started and ended. But at least the moonlight came through unobstructed now. Through gaps in the planking he could see silver glints of current and the bunched maroon of coral heads. The bugs thinned out in the breeze. It was almost peaceful. He reached the weird promontory where the bridge just stopped. He looked around a moment, out to the Gulf and back to the muted lights of town, then dared to sit and even to let his legs dangle insouciantly down into nowhere.

Why not? He wasn't in any real danger...was he? He was following Bert's plan, and Bert was his friend, and Bert was loyal. Then again, Bert was also friends—older friends, Mafia friends—with Tony Totes, who'd been getting jerked around and had good cause to be ticked off. Then there was the heartbroken Ralphie, Tony's right-hand guy. Did Bert also owe loyalty to him? What if there was a hierarchy that put Mob loyalties above all others? What if Bert himself was being squeezed by way too many obligations and had to make a painful choice?

Richie tried to push the unsettling thought away. He trusted Bert. Bert had never let him down. Just the same, he felt a milky unease starting to spread from his spine to the backs of his legs and he decided it might be wiser to move back from the edge and stand somewhere closer to the middle of the stump of bridge.

THIRTY-FIVE

"**O**h Christ, you again?" said Evan, when Bert, his hands discreetly held behind his back, had climbed the porch steps and called out his name.

The writer opened the inner door but kept the screen between them. He was holding a martini glass by its elegant stem. Judging by the slight droop of his pinwheeling eyes, the drink was not his first. "I really don't like it when people just drop by," he said, "Did it ever occur to you I might be working? Might be busy?"

"Busy wit' the cocktail shaker," Bert observed.

Evan managed one of his anchovy-lipped smiles. "Part of my process. The really efficient laborer will saunter to his task surrounded by a wide halo of ease and leisure."

"Shakespeare again? Some Pope?"

"Thoreau. So what are you wasting my time with now?"

"Well, since you are clearly udderwise engaged wit' a host a pressin' matters, I'll be brief. You're comin' to a meetin'."

"Meeting? At this hour? What kind of meeting?"

"Whaddya want, a fuckin' agenda? And who's wastin' whose time now?"

"Well, listen—"

He got no farther in the protest because Bert, with a measured and unemphatic swing of his arm, had brought the gun forward and was holding it trained at the martini glass. "Evan, do I gotta shoot the olive out and make a mess or are ya gonna be reasonable and come along?"

The younger man looked through the gauzy screen at the blurred muzzle of the .38 and his hand began to shake. A bit of his drink sloshed over the rim.

Bert said, "Relax, relax. The gun, it's just parta *my* process. But I'll tell ya what. Act o'mercy. Bring the beverage along but put it in a sippy cup or somethin'. I don't want gin on my upholstery."

Back at the car, Ralphie climbed out and made the writer sit in the middle of the back seat. Tony swiveled around and looked across his shoulder at the new arrival. Seeming confused, he said, "Richie? What the hell were you doin' in that house?"

Darla sighed and said, "Dad, that isn't Richie. That's Evan. Evan inside Evan's house."

Tony, accustomed to being the person in charge, shook his head and said, "Don't be ridiculous. That's been Richie since day one. Why can't any of you people get it right?"

♣ ♣ ♣

They continued on toward the Old Pier Inn to pick up Harry. Harry didn't want to be picked up.

When Bert and Ralphie barged into his room, the author was smoking the last of his Cuban panatelas on his waterfront deck and he made it quite clear he was happy where he was.

"Nice for you," said Bert, "but you're comin' to a meetin' wit' us."

"No I'm not."

"Yes you are."

"No I'm not," he said again. With a pinky, he casually flicked away a length of ash. "Look, I deal with Tony. Directly. Exclusively. What the rest of you guys do, it has nothing to do with me."

Bert said, "*Au contraire*, it has everything to do with you." Along with this flourish of French, he also flourished the revolver. Harry didn't seem too impressed with either.

"So what are you going to do, old man? Shoot me? Here? I don't think so. Put that antique away before you rupture yourself."

Bert chose not to. He kept the gun pointed at the glowing tip of the cigar. It made a vivid target.

Unwisely, Harry stayed on offense. He turned toward Ralphie. "So this meeting you're so hot to drag me to, what's it all about? Probably picking up the pieces from the mess you made with the beating. How badly you fucked up. You think I don't know? You think Tony didn't tell me?"

He gave the big man a smirk, which was one more insult than Ralphie could digest. He flashed Bert a look. Bert gave him a nod. He stepped over to Harry, reached down, grabbed him by his shirt-front, yanked him to his feet, then delivered a tremendous head-butt that brought the full weight and hardness of his skull down onto the bridge of Harry's nose. He let go of the shirt and gave a light push, and suddenly the author was sitting down again, though without the panatela, which had dropped from his hand and lay smoking a few feet away.

He wasn't sure if his nose was broken but he could feel his sinuses overflowing and his cheekbones throbbing as if trying to spit out his eyeballs. Struggling to hold onto his composure, he brought a handkerchief to his face and said, "You're going to be very sorry you did that, Ralphie."

"Maybe. It was worth it."

"You forgot your place. You're just Tony's go-fer. I'm his friend."

Bert considered that a moment, then said, "Well, I know ya used to be. But ya sure ya wanna play that card? Has a waya wearin' thin. Anyway, you'll have a chance to tell your side a the story. So why don't we mosey along before there's any more unpleasantness?"

THIRTY-SIX

Nacho kept spinning and spinning on the console as Bert pulled away from the curb and headed up the Keys.

The happy dog had never seen the old Caddy so jam-packed before, never sniffed it so replete with fascinating smells. There was the juniper tang of Evan's gin and the sweet, rank remnants of Harry's cigar; there was Darla's passionfruit shampoo and the musk of Ralphie's simmering anger and a redolence of garlic from Tony's pasta dinner, all mixed in with the chihuahua's most beloved smell of all, the intoxicating blend of moth balls and mildew that clung to his master's clothing. The little creature's whiskers twitched and quivered with every richly-laden breath.

The humans crammed together in the back seat weren't nearly as happy. Darla, not wanting to rub legs with Evan, had one hip propped on an armrest. Evan, still panicked from the sight of a gun, took spasmodic little nips from his sippy cup. Harry brooded on his grievance and occasionally dabbed real or imagined blood from his nostrils. Early in the ride, he complained to Tony that Ralphie had hit him. Not wanting to play referee just then, Tony told him he'd probably deserved it. Harry stayed silent after that. Ralphie crossed his arms against his chest and smiled inwardly. Maybe his day was finally getting better.

Traffic was light and, even with Bert driving, it didn't take long to reach the turnoff from the highway. The honky-tonk neon glare of US 1 died out within two blocks, giving way to shabby precincts where spindly trees struggled to sink roots into soil that was mainly sand and bits of coral. Rusty boat trailers leaned at random angles in scrubby yards; fallen fronds and storm-blown leaves were piled up on tin roofs that sagged in the middle like failed soufflés. Moment by moment the houses thinned out and the pavement narrowed until there was nothing left except the dead-end path that led to the bridge.

Bert stopped the car. The clamor of insects could be heard even with the windows closed. Tony commented that it was a hell of a place to hold a meeting. Bert assured him it would serve the purpose. He put Nacho on his leash and climbed out from underneath the steering wheel. People billowed forth from the back seat as if they were made of foam that had been folded up too long; they burgeoned into the open air, stretched their shoulders, kicked out their legs. Evan nursed his gin and shook.

Straining at the leash, Nacho led the way into the undergrowth. Lizards slunk away. Crows cackled and egrets rustled at the tops of the trees that swallowed up the moonlight. Now and then there was the rending sound of fabric being shredded by a thorn or a muffled curse as someone was tripped up by a root. The air smelled of sulfur from the foul tea of fallen foliage slowly rotting in brackish water. Up ahead, the trees thinned out and the snaggled boards of the ruined barricade hung limp on broken hinges.

From his lonely vantage on the bridge, Richie fretted about Mob alliances as the others emerged into the moonlight like a ragtag platoon that had survived a jungle skirmish, inching along what was left of the roadway, Nacho sniffing at each dubious board before venturing his tiny leap across it. Bert wagged his gun around to keep the group together but no one seemed inclined to stray. There was nowhere to go, just mosquitoes and scorpions on one side, rushing water and patient barracudas on the other.

Lumbering along with balled-up fists, Ralphie sized up his rival as the distance closed between them. He judged him to be nothing special. Sneeringly, he said to Darla, "So that's him? That's the guy?"

Darla said nothing.

Ralphie said, "Doesn't look like much."

"Please don't hurt him."

"Leverage, Darla. Leverage."

When the seven people and the dog had finally clustered up in the middle of the bridge, Bert, sounding somewhere between a country lawyer and a television emcee, took charge. "Okay," he said. "Nice to get us all together. Long overdue. Lotta misunderstandin's that could use some clearin' up. Maybe some wrongs to be righted. An' I propose that maybe the best waya cuttin' through the bullshit and gettin' to the honest truth would be to play a kinda game."

Harry put his hands on his hips and said, "Game? For Christ's sake, Tony, are we really going to let this mummy—"

"Shut up a minute and let's hear what he has to say."

"Thank you, Tony, for that vote a confidence. So, as I was sayin', we'll play a game, and accordin 'to the rules, which I am right now makin 'up, our three writers heah will be the hopeful contestants, and the resta us'll be the judges. And just to make it innerestin', our contestants'll stand at the enda the bridge, say three steps in, wit' their backs to the water. They will be asked a few questions. If, inna sole discretion a the judges, their answer is deemed to be bullshit, they will be required to take one step back. Same rules apply t'everybody. No favorites. What could be more fair?"

Harry said, "Look, this is utter nonsense."

Tony said, "Whatcha so afraid of, Harry? Do like he says."

For a moment no one moved. Fast current gurgled and sucked beneath the roadway. Nacho sniffed at rotting boards. Evan clung to his sippy cup. Richie reached out for Darla's eyes while trying to dodge Ralphie's.

Bert wagged the gun at people's feet and said, "Contestants will take their places, please."

Harry sent Tony an exasperated glance.

Tony just said, "Move."

The writers shuffled into their positions, elbowing for breathing space. Moonlight tinseled their hair and put a feverish sheen on their foreheads.

Bert turned first toward the quailing figure nursing the last of his martini. "Okay," he said, "let's start wit' you, Shakespeare. Why don't you tell us what your real name is and how you make your livin'."

Through a jaw clenched to quiet the chattering of his teeth, he said, "Evan Briggs. I write novels. I used to write my own. They didn't sell. Now I ghostwrite other people's."

"Yeah, mine!" expostulated Harry.

"It ain't your turn to talk," Ralphie told him.

"Yeah," said Bert, "let's keep it civil." Returning to Evan, he said, "But you ain't been workin' on a novel lately, have ya?"

"No. I've been working on a memoir. Tony's memoir."

Darla said, "While pretending to be somebody who actually knows what he's doing when it comes to writing memoirs."

Evan looked down at his feet and at the black water flashing by beneath the splintered planking. "Yes."

Bert said, "And d'ya think that was fair to Tony?"

Evan twitched then said, "Well..."

"Lemme remind ya," Bert went on, "that a bullshit answer earns ya a blind step backwards."

"Well, no, I guess it wasn't fair."

"Damn straight it wasn't fair," said Tony. "Wasted my time. Lied to my face. There's consequences for shit like that."

Soothingly, Bert said, "We'll get to consequences. For now, we're still workin' on truth."

He nodded toward Richie. "Your turn."

"Name's Richie Delinco. I write memoirs. For certain types of guys—"

"Mob guys," Darla put in. "You can say it. It's not a dirty word, considering the company."

"Okay, Mob guys."

Bert said, "'Cept lately ya been workin' on a novel instead. Is that correct?"

"Yes. The book that Evan's under contract for. I thought it might be fun to take a crack at it."

"Fun?" said Harry. "Fun?!"

Ralphie told him to shut up.

Richie answered the question anyway. "Yeah, I thought it would be easy. I mean, let's face it, the writing's nothing special."

"Nothing special? You amateur son of a bitch."

"Take it easy, Harry," Tony said.

To Richie, Bert said, "You thought it would be easy. Just crankin' out bestsellers. Ya still think it's easy?"

"I don't know. I haven't gotten very far."

"'Course he hasn't," Ralphie said. "Been too busy chasin' other people's girlfriends."

Darla said, "He didn't chase me, Ralphie. I chased him."

The big man chose not to hear that. "An' meanwhile," he went on, "this guy's just as big a part of the lyin' and jerkin' us around as Evan is, but Evan's took a beating, and Harry's took a head-butt, and this Richie guy who on top of it has been messin' wit' my girlfriend, has totally got off scot-free so far. That just don't seem right to me."

"A fair point," Bert conceded. The concession did nothing good for Richie's peace of mind. "But meanwhile, let's hear from the guy who's back from the dead. Your name, please?"

Harry said, "Come on, Bert, cut the crap. Everybody knows my name."

"Check back in a few years. That mighta changed. But okay, we'll dispense wit' the formalities and go straight to a question. Some years ago, you ran out on a buncha debts, including a whopper to Tony heah, and pretended to be dead. Why'd'ya do that, Harry?"

"Because I had no choice."

Bert scratched his cheek with the muzzle of the gun. "'Scuse me," he said, "but that strikes me as bullshit. You did have a choice. You coulda sucked it up, deprived yourself a little and tried at least to do the right thing." He glanced over at Tony. "Whaddya think? It strike you as bullshit, too?"

Tony nodded. So did Ralphie and Darla.

"Take a step back," said Bert.

Harry didn't move.

Bert pointed the revolver at the author's right big toe. "Do I gotta shoot your foot off? Give ya gangrene or some shit?"

Harry stepped back gingerly. Nacho gave a nervous bark.

Tony said, "And while we're onna subject, I got a question about that old debt, too. So you come back and try to maneuver me into gettin' rid of one of these workin' stiffs for your convenience, and you dangle over me this promise of payin' back three million bucks. Did you ever believe, even for a second, that you'd really do that, Harry? That you'd be able to? That you'd choose to?"

"Well...sure, Tony. Over time. Not all at once. But over time."

Tony looked at Bert and said, "I think that backs 'im up another step."

The others all agreed.

Harry said, "Now listen—"

Bert waggled the gun and said, "Ya got one more lie to go, my friend."

Harry felt for something solid with his toe and inched back a tiny step. The chihuahua whimpered from deep down in its throat.

Bert took a moment to look up at the sky. A light haze had put a cottony fuzz and shimmer on the stars. "Beautiful evenin', ain't it?"

No one else offered an opinion.

"Okay," the old man calmly went on, "so let's see where things stand right now. Harry's in some trouble. Richie's maybe getting off too easy. Evan's drunk. But our most basic problem is that we got three writers for two slots. Kind of a musical chairs scenario. Cruel game, as Ralphie and I have discussed on a previous occasion. So who gets the slots? Ya could say that Harry gave up his by pretendin' to be dead. But ya could also say that Evan and Richie ain't legit, since the swappin' thing put 'em inta slots that ain't really theirs ta begin wit'. Then there's the pesky question a Tony's missin' three million—"

"Ah, leave the goddamn money out of it," Tony interrupted. He was speaking to Bert but he never took his eyes off Harry. "Fuck the money. I never really expected to get it back. Stupid me, I bought a friendship wit' that money. Got a shitty deal."

Darla moved closer to her father and took his arm.

Bert sucked his gums then said, "Okay, ixnay onna money part. I guess that somewhat simplifies the landscape. But we still gotta deal wit' the question of whadda we do wit' the guy who's left wit'out a slot? Do we let him hang around and maybe make more trouble downa road? Go squealin' to the publisher, bitchin' to the papers, whatever? Or do we just eliminate the odd guy out while we happen to be standin' inna perfect place to get it done?"

Darla said, "Eliminate?"

Bert said, "Yeah, eliminate. Remove. Subtract."

"As in kill?"

"Guess that's what it comes down ta. Do the math."

"I get the math" she said, "but maybe there's another way to subtract somebody. Less messy. Just as good. I mean, none of this was a problem when Harry was still in Finland and the whole world thought he was dead. Maybe it's enough just to ship him back there."

Bert thought it over. "Innerestin' concept. I guess Finland might be pretty much as good as dead. Outa touch. Forgotten. No trouble t'anyone. Whadda you think, Tony?"

His eyes still glued to Harry's, he said, "Wouldn't give me total satisfaction but I've kinda stopped expectin' that. Would save some worry about a body showin' up. I could maybe get on board with it."

"Except for one problem," Harry said. "I'm not going back there. No way. Ever."

Ralphie said, "What makes ya think it's up to you?"

Harry looked from face to face, desperate for an ally, and his clammy skin glowed purple in the moonlight. His suave voice thinned out to cajoling then to pleading. "Tony, you wouldn't do that to me, right? Send me back there to sit in the dark? Be a nobody. Not even have a name."

The other man just stared at him.

"Come on, Tony. We've been friends forever, for Christ's sake. Don't do this to me. Please. I won't go, Tony. I won't do it. I'd rather die."

The brave words hung above the bridge for just an instant before being carried away by the breeze and the rushing water.

Very mildly, Bert the Shirt said, "Ya sure?"

Harry didn't answer.

Bert took a very slow step forward as he smoothly raised the .38 and pointed it at the author's chest. "It ain't a rhetorical question, Harry. So answer it. Are ya sure?"

Harry's lips moved but he didn't get to speak. He was leaning back, away from the slow thrust of the gun, when a jagged-edged board gave way beneath his weight. It broke not with a crisp crack, but with the soggy surrender of something that had spent a long time rotting, like a spoiled friendship that had festered for years and collapsed the first time it was truly tested. The falling man pinwheeled his arms and flexed his knees in a losing quest for balance. He teetered, swayed, groped at the unsupporting air, then, with the agonized unfolding of the inevitable, he toppled backwards, screaming and flailing. He hit the water piece by piece, almost like a Buick. The surface held his silhouette for some fraction of a second. Then he slipped beneath the surge and the hole he'd made in the water knitted itself closed again.

EPILOGUE

Okay, Richie here, just wanting to assure you that Harry didn't drown or get torn to shreds by barracudas.

Rather, he was tumbled in the current for a couple of hundred yards then spat out into an eddy where he grabbed a mangrove root and dragged himself through the muck to shore. Nacho sniffed him out through the undergrowth and led the rest of us to the reeking puddle where he lay coughing up phlegm and fetid water through his ravaged sinuses. Ralphie, decent in spite of himself, bent low and helped him to his feet. Mud ran down his clothes like candle wax. Bert stood as close as he could stand without wetting his Italian loafers.

Showing the gun, the old man said, "Looked like a nasty slip, Harry. But hopefully ya've had a nice swim and a little time to think things through. So I'll ask ya one last time. What'll it be? Death or Finland?"

Wheezing, his breath still sputtering, finding sympathy in no one's eyes, the soaked man managed a melancholy and self-mocking smile. "Helsinki doesn't seem so bad right now."

"A mature decision," said Bert. "Okay wit' everyone?"

The others nodded.

By way of adjourning the meeting, Bert pointed the gun skyward and pulled the trigger. Nothing happened except for a sharp dry click. He did it five more times, same outcome. "No bullets," he confessed. "Someone coulda got hurt."

And that pretty much wraps up the story of two ghostwriters in a bar, though there were still details to be worked out, of course.

One of these was how people could be sure that Harry would actually go to Finland, since no one any longer trusted that he would do what he had promised. So Tony, through an acquaintance in the longshoreman's union, secured him a berth in an old tub of a freighter slated for a long slow Atlantic passage and an extended period of off-loading in the Baltic nations. Ralphie saw him to the ship, made sure he got on and did not sneak off again. The big man watched the ugly craft depart and didn't relax his vigilance until it had cleared the Statue of Liberty and was headed toward the Verrazzano Narrows.

With Harry out of the equation, and my and Evan's ill-advised ruse blown to smithereens, both of us got down to writing the books we were supposed to be writing in the first place—and that we now approached with renewed gratitude to have the gigs.

Still, there were complications on both sides. Poor Evan, totally rattled by his beating and his confrontation with Bert's empty gun, went into a paralyzing episode of writer's block. This was a bit surprising, as writer's block tends to afflict people who imagine they're better than they are and therefore take themselves too seriously; mere ghostwriters generally don't fit the profile. But Evan is Evan;

a bit of a diva, let's face it. Last I knew, he was falling way behind on his deadline. Then again, he might have woken up manic one morning, written nonstop for a week or so, and gotten all caught up. I wish him well but I don't see us hanging out much in the future. Too much gin and too much maintenance.

I had a minor setback of my own to deal with. You might remember Ralphie's complaint that I was the only one of the troublesome writers to get off scot-free. Well, that wasn't quite true. On the evening when the big man came to hunt me down at the compound but found the naked yoga class instead, he vented his frustration on my stuff. He smashed my computer, toppled a couple of lamps, and slashed the old floral sofa where Darla and I had leaned against each other and launched into that amazing kiss. Had he somehow sensed her presence on the cushion or was the slashing just a random act? In any case, it struck me as terribly sad that the rejected lover's rage was taken out on innocent, inanimate objects; then again, I'll take property damage over personal injury any day.

Aside from finding a new computer and getting the upholstery repaired—call me sentimental, I wasn't about to let that sofa go—I also felt I had a lot of work to do in earning Tony's trust after the knucklehead conspiracy to deceive him. So, in part to win him over and in part to clear my conscience, I made the grandest gesture I could think of: I offered to write his book for free as a token of apology and respect.

He seemed to appreciate the offer but, to my relief, did not accept. He was too much of an old-school sport to let some poor schnook work for nothing. The only wrinkle was that business was calling him back to New York and I'd have to go north for the interviews. So I rented an airbnb and spent a couple of weeks. I got to like Tony more and more. I saw him as a flawed but well-meaning guy in a world changing faster than he could really keep up with. New rules making his time-honored profession obsolete. A restless wife who left him with a daughter he didn't quite know how to raise. Fancy friends whose standards of loyalty fell way short of his own. In brief, a guy who did his best in life but then was left, at various moments, to wonder why he'd bothered. In other words, a human being. I hope I can write a decent memoir for him.

Did I see Darla while I was in New York? Sure, but not as lovers. As lovers we were one-and-done, and I think we're both okay with that. Wistful but without regrets. For Darla, I think I was a transitional guy. No shame or cynicism in that. Key West showed her that she'd outgrown Ralphie. But what would come next? I think we both sensed that I was not the next big thing for her. A bridge to it, maybe. Hopefully a bridge that someday completes its arc to something dreamy on the other side.

And what was Darla for me? Boy, it's so much harder when it's your own emotions you're trying to describe. I don't think it's a stretch to say I was smitten by her, and still am, since there wasn't time enough in that blink-of-an-eye romance for anything to change. But it was mainly just a lucky accident that we got together. Without the collision on the promenade, we never would have spoken. Frankly, I would have been intimidated by her looks, but also dismissive because she seemed at first like just another tourist. Tourists and locals are separate tribes down here. Always have been, always will be. Still, I expect that, for a while at least, I'll feel a pang every time I bike past the Sno-Cone truck.

Which I do almost every day now that I'm back in Key West. Sometimes I just go for aimless seafront rides to clear my head. Other times I have a destination, namely a certain little bump of Smathers Beach known as Sunset Bluff, where I'm pretty sure to find Bert and Nacho facing toward the western sky. Bert sits in his aluminum chair with the white and yellow nylon straps. Nacho digs sand until he sneezes. If people walk by, Bert talks to them. Always. He doesn't wait to be talked to. He talks. He asks. He shows an interest. He launches into stories, offers streetwise counsel in his own personal vocabulary. That's just who he is.

And it has struck me lately—having played my part in this comedy of errors and fakery—that this simple knack of knowing who you are, and being okay with it, and being that person at every single moment without a fudge or waver, is a surprisingly rare and high achievement. Maybe it only comes with age. A lot of age. Or maybe some few people are just born with a gift for it. For being real. Who knows? I'll ask Bert next time I see him. I'm sure he'll have opinions on the subject.

ABOUT THE AUTHOR

Laurence Shames is the author of eighteen *Key West Capers*, as well as many other works of fiction and nonfiction. As a ghostwriter, he has penned four *New York Times* bestsellers, in four different categories, under four different names. Formerly a columnist for *Esquire* and *The New York Observer*, he has contributed hundreds of articles and essays to publications including *Vanity Fair, Outside, Travel & Leisure*, and *The New York Times Magazine*. His work has been translated into more than a dozen languages, and he is a recipient of the United Kingdom's *Macallan Last Laugh Dagger* for his comic mystery writing.

To learn more, please visit https://laurenceshames.com

Works by Laurence Shames

Key West Capers—
Relative Humidity
Key West Normal
The Paradise Gig
Nacho Unleashed
One Big Joke
One Strange Date
Key West Luck
Tropical Swap
Shot on Location
The Naked Detective
Welcome to Paradise
Mangrove Squeeze
Virgin Heat
Tropical Depression
Sunburn
Scavenger Reef
Florida Straits

Key West Short Fiction—
Chickens

New York & California Novels—
Money Talks
The Angels' Share

Nonfiction—
The Hunger for More
The Big Time

Printed in the USA
CPSIA information can be obtained
at www.ICGtesting.com
LVHW021915020324
773372LV00004B/106

9 798873 975594